Waffles and
Cove Cozy Mystery Series Book 5

By Leena Clover

Chapter 1

Jenny King's cheeks flamed with embarrassment as she observed her friend Heather over the rim of her wine glass.

It was Valentine's weekend and the four couples had met for dinner at The Steakhouse, Pelican Cove's only fancy restaurant. Jenny, Heather and Molly were close friends. Jenny considered Jason Stone a friend too. He was the only lawyer in Pelican Cove and was currently dating another lawyer from the city. He had pursued Jenny for a while after she came to live in Pelican Cove. But Jenny had made her choice. She looked up into the blue eyes of her date. Adam Hopkins, the sheriff of Pelican Cove smiled back at her.

Heather Morse cuddled with a man much older than herself. She had been dating Gianni Costa, Dr. Gianni Costa, for the past few months. The flamboyant fiftyish man had set up shop as soon as he moved to the small seaside town. He flirted outrageously with his patients, most of whom were older ladies who liked being flattered by the silver-tongued Casanova.

Jenny watched as Heather engaged in behavior her grandmother would not approve of. Adam nudged her and cleared his throat.

"What did you do last night?" Jenny asked her friend Molly.

"Chris and I had a romantic dinner at home. We didn't want to spend our first Valentine's Day at a restaurant."

"We went for a canoe ride after that," Chris beamed, looking lovingly at Molly. "Molly loves those."

Jason's date spoke up.

"We went to a hot new restaurant in town. I know the chef personally. He's about to get his first Michelin star."

"The weekend's going great, then," Jenny said happily. "Don't forget you are all coming to Seaview tomorrow."

"Isn't it a bit cold for a barbecue?" Kandy, the city lawyer, asked.

"We'll have a fire going in the pit," Jason assured her. "Seaview is a great place to be, any time of the year."

Jenny still couldn't believe she was the proud owner of a sea facing mansion. Dumped by her husband of twenty years, she had grabbed her aunt's invitation like a lifeline and come to visit her in the small seaside town of Pelican Cove. A barrier island off the coast of Virginia, Pelican Cove was the perfect place to lick her wounds. Jenny's aunt Star had let her wallow for a few weeks and urged her to start working at the local café. Neither of them knew she was going to be a big success. Jenny had started baking and cooking with the local produce and turned the Boardwalk Café around. Tourists flocked to the café to taste the delectable treats Jenny created on a regular basis.

"Your parties are legendary, Jenny," Heather nodded. "Gianni and I can't wait for tomorrow."

"Have you settled in at Seaview?" Molly asked Jenny.

Jenny had been charmed by the big three story house adjoining her aunt's cottage. She had bought the house with her divorce settlement and spent a big sum of money renovating it. The discovery of a skeleton in her garden had been unexpected. But Jenny had soldiered on and moved into the house with her aunt.

"It's a great house," Jenny told her friend. "I'm loving it more each day."

"And having Adam there helps," Heather remarked with a wink.

When Jenny first came to Pelican Cove, Adam and Jason had both fallen for her. Jenny found herself pursued by two handsome, eligible men. They were as different as chalk and cheese. Jenny had chosen to date Adam, the more unpredictable of the two.

"Adam's living on the third floor," Jenny said curtly. "It's not what you think."

"Why do you protest so much?" Heather pouted. "I don't care where he lives. By the way, as far as appearances go, you two live in the same house."

Adam grew uncomfortable. He tucked a finger in his collar and tried to loosen it. His roof had fallen in a few weeks ago and he had been forced to move out. Jenny had insisted he stay at Seaview until his house was fixed. Their living arrangement had set tongues wagging. Jenny told him she didn't care what people said.

"Let's not talk about 'appearances', Heather," Jenny fumed.

"Simmer down, you two," Jason Stone said lightly. He gave Jenny a knowing look. "Are you denying you and Adam are a couple?"

"Jenny's just being a good friend," Adam protested. "I would have come and lived with you, Jason. But you didn't offer."

Dr. Gianni Costa looked bored with the conversation.

"Basta!" he exclaimed. "How about another round of drinks? They are on me."

He ordered an expensive bottle of wine for the table.

Dr. Costa had plenty of money and he believed in spending it.

"I am looking forward to this party at your home," he told Jenny. "I want to see this spot where they found that skeleton."

"There's nothing to look at there," Jenny said bluntly. "We put a water fountain on the spot."

The bottle of wine arrived and Dr. Costa and Heather drank most of it. He insisted on getting the check.

"My treat," he told the others. "You can pay next time."

Heather stumbled out of the restaurant with the good doctor, both of them swaying a bit.

"I hope you're not driving," Adam said anxiously. "Can I give you a ride somewhere?"

He had opted to be the designated driver for the group.

"We want to walk home," Heather slurred. "It's such a beautiful night."

"Not more beautiful than you, my pet," Gianni Costa murmured.

He clutched Heather's hand in his and waved goodbye

to the group.

"Ciao friends," he cried with a big smile on his face. "Heather and I have our own little party planned."

He took a couple of steps and stumbled. He let out a burp and Heather giggled.

"You're totally wasted, Heather," Jenny clucked, shaking her head. "Maybe we should see you home safely."

"I'm going to Gianni's," Heather whispered in her ear. "You go have fun with Adam."

There was another round of goodbyes and the group finally dispersed. Adam drove Chris and Molly home.

"You think she'll be alright?" Molly asked Jenny.

"She's thirty five, Molls, not thirteen," Jenny said with a sigh. "I think she can take care of herself."

"Heather's changed a lot, hasn't she?" Chris muttered.

Chris Williams had been in love with Heather Morse since third grade. Everyone knew they had an understanding. Heather had shocked everyone the previous summer by deciding to date other people. Chris had found himself falling for Molly, the shy, soft spoken librarian. Chris and Molly found they had a deep connection. They were very much in love.

"What does Heather see in Gianni?" Jenny wondered, her frustration evident in her voice.

Jenny and Adam watched a movie after getting home. Adam had let her pick Casablanca in honor of the special weekend.

Jenny hummed a tune as she mixed some batter for her special waffles the next morning. The café opened a bit later than usual on Sunday. Most of her regular customers turned up for breakfast, eager to indulge in whatever sinful treat Jenny dished up.

Jenny greeted Captain Charlie as she threw open the doors of the café. He was her favorite customer, always first in line when the café opened.

"Got those waffles?" he asked her. "I've been dreaming about having them for breakfast."

Jenny brought out a platter with hot waffles drizzled with a fresh berry sauce. Captain Charlie smacked his lips as he cut into his food.

"Delicious!" he pronounced after the first bite.

"Do you want chocolate sauce too?" Jenny asked him. "Or some chocolate covered strawberries? I saved some for you."

Jenny chatted with people as she offered them a choice of fresh berry sauce or melted chocolate to top their waffles. Some opted for both.

Jenny's friends began walking in around eleven. They were an odd group of women, young and old. Betty Sue Morse, Heather's grandmother, was the unopposed leader of the pack. She was a force to reckon with even in her eighties. Jenny's aunt Star and café owner Petunia Clark formed the rest of the old guard. Jenny, Molly and Heather provided the young blood, although at 45, Jenny was much older than Heather and Molly. The ladies called themselves the Magnolias and met at the café every morning.

Betty Sue was busy with her knitting as usual. All the Magnolias were dressed warmly because they wanted to sit out on the deck. The café's deck sat right on the sand, facing the Atlantic Ocean.

"How was Valentine's Day?" Betty Sue's voice boomed. "I hope you girls are behaving yourself?"

Molly blushed prettily, making Petunia and Star laugh.

"Chris and I can't wait for the barbecue at Jenny's," Molly said. "You are coming, aren't you, Betty Sue?"

"Of course I am," Betty Sue nodded. "I am looking forward to it."

"Why don't you invite John?" Star asked.

John Newbury was Betty Sue's estranged husband.

Betty Sue turned red at the mention of his name.

"Why would I do that?" she sputtered.

"It is Valentine's weekend," Star teased. "Don't you want to spend some time with your honey?"

The older ladies proceeded to tease Betty Sue mercilessly. Jenny thought it was cute how Betty Sue broke out in a sweat every time her husband was mentioned.

"Where's Heather?" Molly asked innocently.

Jenny shook her head meaningfully and tried to warn Molly. But Betty Sue had already heard her.

"She's fast asleep in her bed," Betty Sue complained. "Wouldn't budge. I had to take Tootsie for her walk myself." She looked at Jenny and Molly inquiringly. "How come you two look so fresh? Didn't Heather get any sleep at all last night?"

Jenny hastily changed the subject.

"Did Chris give you a gift, Molly?"

Molly leaned forward and showed them a new pair of earrings she was wearing. The ladies exclaimed over the heart shaped jewelry.

"Did Adam get you anything?" Molly asked.

Jenny smiled and shook her head. She hadn't expected fancy jewelry but she had hoped Adam would get her a memento of some kind. He had brought her breakfast in bed, along with a posy of her favorite roses from the garden at Seaview. Jenny told herself she didn't need fancy gifts. She had received enough of those from her ex-husband. They had meant nothing in the end.

She felt her heart skip a beat and looked around. Adam strode along the beach and ran up the café steps.

"Hello ladies," he greeted them.

His eyes softened as they met Jenny's. Adam looked apologetic. Jenny knew that look. She braced herself for what Adam would say next.

"Where is Heather?" Adam asked Betty Sue.

"Don't ask!" Betty Sue said with a roll of her eyes. "She's sleeping like the dead."

"Funny you should say that," Adam said tersely.

The Magnolias were staring at him now.

"Spit it out," Star said. "You have some bad news."

"Gianni died in his sleep last night."

A collective gasp went through the group.

"Are you sure?" Molly burst out. "Maybe he's just passed out."

"I am sure, Molly," Adam said with a sigh. "I need to talk to Heather."

Jenny sat down with a thump. They had all seen Heather go home with Gianni Costa. She had probably been the last person to see him alive. One of the last people, Jenny corrected herself.

"How did he die?" she asked Adam fearfully.

Adam's brow furrowed as he answered her.

"It's too early to say, but looks like he was drugged."

Betty Sue had put her knitting down for a change. She had been trying to get a word in.

"What does Heather have to do with that flashy doctor? She barely knew him."

Chapter 2

Jenny walked to the police station with a wicker basket on her arm. The lunch rush at the café had died down and she was off to have lunch with Adam. She had packed chicken rolls and slices of carrot cake.

Adam Hopkins sat with one leg propped up on a chair. He was a veteran who had been deployed in war zones. He had been shot in the leg and still struggled with the old injury. He had a mercurial temper which flared every time his leg bothered him.

"How are you, Jenny?" He had a special smile for her.

Although Adam and Jenny lived in the same house, their work schedules were such that they barely saw each other.

"Hungry?" Jenny asked, unpacking the basket.

Adam took a big bite of the roll and gave her a thumbs up.

"Yum! What is it?"

"It's a new Asian style chicken recipe I am trying out," Jenny explained, taking a dainty bite of her own sandwich.

They made some small talk while they ate. Adam finally polished off the last bite of cake and wiped his mouth with a tissue. He gave Jenny a grave look.

"I got some news about Mrs. Bones."

'Mrs. Bones' was the nickname Jenny and the girls had assigned the skeleton that had been discovered in Jenny's backyard. For a long time, Jenny and her friends had believed that the skeleton belonged to a missing girl from the area. That theory had been shot down. Now Jenny suspected something else.

"Tell me, quick."

"It's a woman, as you already know," Adam began. "A woman about fifty years old. She's been buried for thirty some years."

"Anything else?" Jenny asked with bated breath.

"They found a broken collar bone, probably a childhood injury."

Jenny's eyes shone with excitement.

"Finally, something we can verify. Betty Sue might know about this."

"Do you really believe that's Lily?" Adam asked.

Jenny nodded sadly. The tragic history of Seaview

flashed before her eyes. Seaview had been home to the Davis family, one of the pioneer families of Pelican Cove. Old man Davis had lived there with his entire family. A big storm had wiped out most of them, leaving only his daughter Lily, his son's wife and his grandson alive. Ann Davis, the son's wife, had taken her baby and Lily and moved away. Lily came back thirty years later with her husband and children. But tragedy struck again. Lily lost her daughter to a freak virus. Then Lily herself disappeared one night. The general impression in town had been that Lily abandoned her family and ran away with another man. As more information surfaced about the skeleton, Jenny was sure Lily had met an untimely end.

"She's the only fiftyish woman who went missing from these parts," Jenny reminded Adam. "And no one heard from her again."

"You know what you are implying?" Adam asked, leaning back in his chair.

He pulled a bottle of pills from a drawer and tried to unscrew the top. Jenny took the bottle and opened it for him.

"Lily was killed," Jenny said flatly. She looked impatient as Adam popped a couple of pills in his mouth and washed them down with a sip of water. "That's obvious, isn't it? She didn't bury herself in my garden."

"You may be right," Adam continued. "Someone bashed her head in."

"Poor Lily," Jenny mumbled.

"One more mystery for you to solve, huh?" Adam teased.

"Aren't you going to tell me to stay out of it?" Jenny asked with surprise.

Adam didn't like anyone meddling into police business. He and Jenny were often at odds with each other because of it.

"It's a cold case," Adam shrugged. "There's not much anyone can do."

"But Lily deserves justice!" Jenny argued.

Lily's son had died the previous year. Her husband was in a senior home in Texas. No one was going to come and ask the police to find Lily's murderer.

"Maybe you can do something about it," Adam said mildly.

"Are you actually giving me your blessing?" Jenny asked incredulously.

"Just be careful," Adam warned, "and keep me updated."

Jenny walked to the seafood market to shop for dinner. Chris Williams filled her order. They chatted for some time and Jenny walked home. Dinner was a lively affair with her aunt's special friend Jimmy Parsons joining them. Jimmy had been better known as the town drunk for several years. He had recently turned his life around and was dating her aunt. He spent a lot of his time at Seaview.

Jenny and Adam went for their usual walk on the beach after dinner. Jenny threw a ball for Tank, Adam's yellow Labrador. Tank had moved into Seaview with Adam. He adored Jenny and could be seen following her through the house, his tail wagging.

The next morning, Jenny couldn't wait to meet the Magnolias. She baked a fresh tray of banana nut muffins and had the coffee ready. Betty Sue arrived, her needles clacking with force as she took in the guests at the café. Heather followed behind, looking morose.

"How are you holding up, Heather?" Jenny asked.

Heather's eyes filled up.

"How would you be doing in my place?"

"I didn't know you were that close," Jenny sympathized. "I mean, sure, we know you had some fun with him. But did you actually care about him?"

"Of course I did," Heather cried. "Gianni made me happy."

Betty Sue refused to acknowledge Heather's connection to the dead doctor.

"Stop mooning around, girl," she ordered. "Pour me a cup of coffee."

Molly stumbled into the café, holding on to her Coke-bottle glasses. Star wasn't far behind.

"I can smell spring in the air," Star said as she doodled a drawing on a paper napkin.

Star was an artist who painted landscapes and seascapes. The tourists loved her work. She had a gallery in town and Jenny had helped her set up a website. Star worked hard in winter and spring to replenish her catalog. The tourist season would ramp up soon.

"Spring Fest is around the corner," Betty Sue reminded them. "We need to work on it."

"Barb's back early this year," Star observed.

Barb Norton was a local woman who took an active part in all the town events. She spent winter in Florida with her daughter but got back in time to organize the spring festival. The Magnolias liked to give her the cold shoulder but they had to admit she was resourceful.

"She'll be around soon enough," Petunia said softly.

"Can we talk about Mrs. Bones?" Jenny butted in. She had been trying to find the right moment to talk about Lily. "Did Lily ever have any accidents as a child, Betty Sue?"

Betty Sue paused from her knitting and narrowed her eyes.

"Lily was a hellion. My Daddy was quite strict with me but old man Davis let Lily roam around the island. She swam with the watermen's kids and could outrow them any day."

"So you two didn't play together?"

"I'm coming to it," Betty Sue said irritably. "Lily came to visit a lot. We could play in our yard but I wasn't allowed to go out with her."

Jenny wished Betty Sue would get on with her reminisces. She tried to curb her impatience.

"One afternoon, we snuck out and walked to one of the bluffs. Someone had tied a rope swing on an oak. I got sick just looking at it. Lily scrambled up and made me push the swing."

"Is this going anywhere?" Heather asked with a yawn.

Betty Sue barely heard her. She was lost in the

memories of her childhood.

"Lily begged me to push harder every time. We were both yelling, Lily with abandon, me with fright. Suddenly, she flew in the air and crashed to the ground."

"She broke her collar bone, didn't she?" Jenny asked urgently.

Betty Sue's mouth dropped open.

"Don't interrupt, Jenny," Star quipped. "Let her finish."

"She's right," Betty Sue said, pointing a finger at Jenny. "I'll never forget that day. Lily had a nasty scrape on her chin and a broken bone. She was howling for hours. We were both grounded for weeks after that."

"Mrs. Bones has a fractured collar bone," Jenny said softly.

"So there's no doubt it's Lily?" Betty Sue asked sadly.

"It's beginning to look like that," Jenny said, placing her hand on Betty Sue's. "The police might run some more tests. Then we'll know for sure."

Betty Sue's face hardened as she looked at Jenny.

"I want you to clear Lily's name. They didn't just kill

her. They destroyed her reputation."

"I'm going to do my best," Jenny promised her.

"What about Gianni?" Heather wailed. "Aren't you going to find out what happened to him?"

"Gianni Costa died in his sleep," Star snapped. "He had one drink too many."

Petunia seconded Star.

"What kind of doctor was he, anyway? He should have known when to stop."

"He didn't drink that much," Heather argued. "We all drank wine at the restaurant."

"What about after he got home?" Molly asked. "He must have had a few more drinks then."

Heather had no answer for that. She didn't remember much of what had happened after they reached Gianni's home. But she wasn't ready to admit that.

"You're all just bad-mouthing him," Heather insisted. "Jenny needs to find out the truth."

"Hold on, Heather," Jenny protested. "That's not my job. The police will look into it. What do you think I am? Some kind of detective?"

"It won't be the first time you solved a murder," Heather said sullenly.

"That was different," Jenny said.

"She's right," Betty Sue spoke up. "That doctor was a menace. Good riddance, I say."

"Grandma!" Heather cried. "You barely knew him."

"Jenny has her hands full with Mrs. Bones," Molly reiterated.

Heather opened her mouth to argue. A loud voice hailed them from the boardwalk.

"Yooohoooo …"

A short, plump woman scrambled up the café steps.

"Hello Barb," Star drawled. "The Spring Fest committee doesn't meet for three more days."

Barb Norton sat down next to Molly and tried to catch her breath. Jenny offered her a cup of coffee. She took a sip gratefully and looked around at the assembled women.

"Forget the Spring Fest."

"Are you stepping down as Chairperson?" Star asked eagerly. "It's my turn now, anyway."

Barb glared at Star.

"The Spring Fest will go ahead as planned. I am here on important business."

"What's got your panties in a wad?" Betty Sue thundered.

"Dire things are afoot, Betty Sue," Barb Norton said urgently. "We need to gather everyone for an emergency town meeting."

"What's the matter now?" Jenny asked.

Jenny had lived in a city most of her life. Small town politics was new to her. She was still amazed by how the people came together to discuss and dissect every small issue. There was a committee for everything, Jenny had found.

"Our very way of life is being threatened," Barb said dramatically.

She flung a finger at Betty Sue.

"Those Newburys are doing it again. And your husband is responsible."

"What is John doing now?" Betty Sue asked mildly.

"Drugs!" Barb declared, her bosom heaving. "The Newburys are getting into the drug business."

"What nonsense!" Betty Sue dismissed.

Jenny, Heather and Molly shared a swift glance. They were trying hard not to laugh. Barb Norton pounced on them.

"You find this funny?"

"Stop being fanciful, Barb," Star said curtly. "Get to the point."

"The Newburys are planting cannabis in their fields," Barb declared triumphantly. "They are going to sell it too, right here in town. John Newbury signed a lease on that empty store on the corner of Main. Eddie Cotton owns that store. He told me himself."

"Are they opening a medical marijuana dispensary?" Jenny asked.

"I don't care how they sugarcoat it," Barb sniffed. "We cannot have drugs in Pelican Cove."

Chapter 3

Jenny added a generous amount of ground cinnamon to her waffle batter. She added some orange zest to the berries bubbling away on the stove. She was fixing a special batch of her waffles based on Barb Norton's request. The Spring Fest committee had met the previous night but hadn't reached consensus on a single point. Jenny had suggested consulting Mandy. Everyone had agreed to that suggestion.

Mandy James was a consultant the town had hired before. She had helped them win the Prettiest Town in America tag. Jenny was sure she would have plenty of ideas about how to make Spring Fest bigger and better. A conference call had been set up and the ladies were going to gather in the café to talk to Mandy via video conference.

Jenny fussed over arranging the perfect plate of waffles and wished Heather would hurry. Barb wanted a picture of the waffles for the Spring Fest flyers. Jenny also wanted to post the picture on the town's Instagram page.

"Merchandise!" Mandy James said resolutely. "Anything you can think of – t-shirts, tote bags, baseball caps – something for everyone. You make money this year and get free advertising for the next.

And swag! You need to give away swag."

Mandy was on a roll. The Magnolias groaned as Mandy rattled off one suggestion after another. They hadn't missed this aspect of her personality.

"Hold on, Mandy," Jenny said. "Heather's taking notes."

"Aren't you recording this?" Mandy asked.

"We prefer to take notes the old fashioned way," Barb Norton bristled. "Now tell us what this swag is."

Mandy spent a few minutes explaining how they could give away small items like pens or key chains with the town's logo on it.

"Get some big items for the raffle," Mandy ordered. "Everything should have the town's web address on it."

Jenny's mind was working furiously, thinking about ways to spread the word about the Boardwalk Café.

"Why don't we get some special tees printed?" she asked Petunia. "We can put a pretty picture on them, like these waffles, along with our name and address."

"Whatever you think is right, dear," she said uncertainly.

Jenny turned toward the screen and spoke to Mandy.

"What about having a concert on the beach? I know you shot my suggestion down last time, but the Spring Fest seems like a good time for some music."

"That's an excellent idea, Jenny," Mandy approved. "Why don't you start contacting a few bands?"

Barb started working on the waffles while the women threw ideas around.

"You don't know what you are missing," she told Mandy. "When are you coming for a visit? Jenny's come up with plenty of yummy recipes since you left."

"Let me check my calendar," Mandy said seriously. "I will try to make it there for the Spring Fest. No promises, though."

Heather sat with a camera in her lap, staring into space. Molly nudged Jenny and tipped her head at Heather.

"We need to do something," she hissed.

"Looks like she's really grieving for Gianni," Jenny shrugged. "We need to get her out of this funk."

"How about a trip to the city?" Molly asked. "Let's catch a movie and get her favorite dinner."

The girls decided to talk to Heather after the

conference call ended. Barb Norton made Jenny fix a fresh plate of waffles and ordered Heather to take a few dozen photos from all angles. She went off on another mission after that. The girls finally heaved a sigh of relief.

Heather didn't want to go to the city.

"How can I enjoy a movie when my sweetie just died?" she wailed. "How heartless do you think I am?"

"How about a visit to the spa?" Jenny offered. "My treat."

"Have you been biting these?" Molly asked, picking up Heather's hand and peering at her nails.

Vanity won and Heather agreed to tag along to the spa. Molly chattered continuously as Jenny drove off the bridge that connected the island of Pelican Cove to the mainland. Heather stared out of the window, tears streaming down her cheeks. Jenny gave her a worried glance.

"You need to pull yourself together, Heather."

Heather pulled out a few tissues from a box on the dashboard. She blew her nose and nodded wordlessly.

"I didn't realize you were so attached to him," Jenny continued.

"Gianni cared about me. I might have had a future with him."

Jenny bit her lip and forced herself to stay quiet. Had Heather really been thinking about marrying a man fifteen years her senior? She thought of the flamboyant doctor with his flashy clothes and diamond earring. His shirt had been unbuttoned every time Jenny met him, exposing his hairy chest.

"You'll find someone else," Molly soothed.

Molly's comment didn't go down well. Jenny believed Heather hadn't forgiven Molly for hooking up with Chris.

"You take as much time as you need, Heather," Jenny said diplomatically. "We can put up your profile on that dating site again."

"It's a mobile app," Heather corrected her. "No one uses websites anymore."

"Why don't we take a new photo after our spa visit, hmm?" Jenny soothed.

Heather seemed to rally around a bit after that. They chose a three hour package at the spa. Jenny found herself relaxing after a long time as she let herself be scrubbed and massaged. They went to Heather's favorite restaurant overlooking the Chesapeake Bay for a late lunch.

"I'm starving," Heather said. "I'm getting the blackened sea bass."

The girls ordered different entrees and switched them around after a few bites. Jenny couldn't resist ordering the bourbon pecan pie for dessert.

"Thanks for doing this, girls," Heather said on the way back. "I almost feel human."

Jenny squeezed Heather's hand.

"We're here for you, sweetie. Just let us know what you need."

Jason was sitting out on the patio with Star when Jenny got home. She was happy to see him.

"Jason!" she exclaimed happily. "We hardly see you anymore."

Jason sprang up and hugged Jenny. "You're glowing, Jenny."

"After what I spent at that spa, I better," Jenny joked. "What brings you here?"

"Kandy's busy with a case," he told them. "And I've cleared my desk too for a change. So I thought I would enjoy an evening at Seaview."

"You're always welcome here," Star said warmly.

She had a soft corner for Jason and preferred him over Adam. She made sure she told Jenny about it plenty of times.

"Is Adam home yet?" Jenny asked.

"He just left," Star said gleefully. "He's working till midnight."

"How's Nick?" Jason asked. "Haven't seen him in a while."

Jenny's son Nick was a sophomore in college. Jenny rubbed a small gold charm that hung around her neck. Nick had gifted her a charm for Mother's Day ever since he was a kid. They hung around Jenny's neck on a chain. She had the habit of rubbing the charms whenever she missed her son.

"He should be here for Spring Fest," Jenny said. "Hopefully even before that."

"Did you hear about John Newbury's plans?" Star asked Jason. "What do you think?"

"I think he's got guts," Jason said. "But the Newburys never cared about the town folk."

"Surely they won't do anything illegal?" Jenny asked, wide eyed.

"Having the law on their side won't be enough," Jason

explained. "Communities around the country have protested against these dispensaries."

"Aren't they supposed to help sick people?" Jenny asked.

Jason let out a sigh.

"The amount of people they can help is less than the ones they can harm, I guess. People are afraid of the ramifications, and rightly so."

They argued over the pros and cons of growing medical cannabis in a small town like Pelican Cove.

"You can be sure of one thing," Star said. "There will be a protest, and a big one. Those Newburys better be ready for it."

Jenny insisted on cooking Jason's favorite pan seared fish in a wine butter sauce. He had brought a bottle of local wine Jenny loved. They lingered over chocolate brownies and ice cream on the patio. Jason had built a fire in the pit. The scent of roses and gardenias perfumed the air. Water gurgled in the stone fountain.

Jenny sighed with pleasure as she looked around her. This was her home now.

The Magnolias were all fired up about the Spring Fest the next day. Star had produced some designs for the festival T-shirts. The ladies pored over them, arguing over which one best represented Pelican Cove.

"I like this one with just the crab," Molly said. "It's simple but elegant."

"I prefer this one," Heather opposed her. "Crab, oyster, sea bass in a basket and the light house and beach in the background. It's all the best of Pelican Cove."

"Did you post that photo of the waffles on Instagram?" Jenny asked, bringing out a plate of warm muffins.

"Already done, Jenny. It has some five thousand likes. Get ready to make plenty of waffles."

Adam Hopkins came in sight, flanked by two men in uniform. He was leaning on his cane heavily, wincing with every step.

"Is your leg bothering you?" Jenny asked with concern. "Have you taken any pain pills this morning?"

Adam gave her a quelling look. He didn't like being fussed over in public.

The two men accompanying Adam had gone to stand beside Heather.

"What are you doing here, boy?" Betty Sue demanded.

"You need to come with us, Heather," Adam said curtly.

Jenny put her arms on her hips and glared at Adam.

"Not again! You are making a habit of this, Adam. I think you like coming here and harassing us."

"Just doing my job," Adam muttered.

"What has my child done?" Betty Sue asked imperiously.

"Heather was seen going home with Gianni Costa the night he died. We need to question her."

"You don't think I hurt Gianni?" Heather asked fearfully. "I cared for him. Very much."

"We can discuss all that in my office," Adam told her. "Let's go."

"Jenny!" Heather's eyes filled with panic as she looked around at the group. "What am I to do?"

"You'll have to go with him," Jenny said with a sigh.

"We are right behind you," Star said, getting up.

Heather looked bewildered as she stood up and followed Adam down the café steps. She kept glancing back at her friends, looking wild eyed.

"I'm calling Jason," Jenny said, rushing inside the café.

Betty Sue Morse had dumped her knitting on the table. She looked ashen. Molly helped her up and the ladies started walking down to the police station. Jenny ran a few steps and caught up with them.

"He'll meet us there," she said breathlessly.

Jason Stone was pacing up and down the police station lobby when they got there.

"She's inside. Don't worry. They can't hold her for long."

"I thought my Heather was rid of that awful man," Betty Sue sobbed.

"Hush, Betty Sue," Jenny warned. "Be careful what you say."

"I'm not afraid of anyone," Betty Sue puffed up. "Least of all, that beau of yours."

Jenny knew Adam had a job to do. His way of carrying out his duties often rubbed her the wrong way. Jenny realized none of that mattered in the present situation. If Heather was in trouble, she would do anything to help her clear her name.

Heather came out of a tiny room an hour later, looking bewildered. The Magnolias surrounded her immediately, throwing all kinds of questions at her.

Heather gently pushed them away and stared at Jenny.

"I need your help, Jenny. Are you going to find out who killed Gianni?"

Chapter 4

Jenny thought about Heather while frosting chocolate cupcakes. Heather had come to mean a lot to her. She was like her baby sister. Jenny resolved to do whatever needed to help Heather. The first step was going to be getting some background information on Dr. Gianni Costa.

Gianni had been in town only a short time. No one knew much about his past. Jenny had looked for his profile on social media the previous night. He had posted some photos of the beaches at Pelican Cove. There were some photos with Heather plastered to his side. But all the photos only went back a few months. There was nothing about his family or his previous life. Jenny had brought her laptop to work. She was going to dig deeper as soon as she got a chance.

Jenny fired up her laptop after lunch and began looking for Gianni Costa. Jenny was surprised when an address showed up for Gianni in Delaware. It was a small town on the coast, roughly a hundred miles from Pelican Cove.

Jenny felt a surge of energy as she spotted a phone number next to the address. She fed the number in her cell phone and crossed her fingers as she hit the green icon that would dial the number.

The phone barely rang twice before it was answered. The woman sounded brusque, as if she was just stepping out of the door.

"Does this number belong to Dr. Gianni Costa?" Jenny asked.

"Who is this?" the woman shot back.

"My name is Jenny King. I live in Pelican Cove."

"Are you Gianni's harpy?"

"Excuse me?" Jenny sputtered.

"Are you that girl he's been hanging out with lately?" the woman asked patiently.

"I'm not," Jenny said firmly. "I'm her friend."

"What do you want?"

"May I know who I am talking to?"

"Gianni's wife. Mrs. Gianni Costa."

The woman's smug tone carried over the phone line. Jenny found herself speechless.

"I didn't know Gianni was married," she finally managed to blurt out.

"You and everyone else, sister!"

"I would like to talk to you about Gianni," Jenny burst out. "Do you think we can meet?"

"You have my address," the woman said in a bored voice. "Give me a call when you are in town."

Jenny hung up. She was still trying to digest the fact that Gianni was married. Had Heather known about it?

Star came into the café's kitchen and flopped down into a chair. Her face was set in a frown.

"Had a fight with Jimmy?" Jenny teased.

"How old do you think I am, girl? Sixteen?" Star was rarely short with her.

"What's wrong, then?" Jenny asked, offering her aunt a freshly frosted cupcake.

Star considered the platter before her and chose one from the center. She took a big bite and licked the frosting off her lips.

"Are you reading minds now?" she asked Jenny.

Jenny waited patiently. She knew her aunt was just trying to buy time.

"There's a new art gallery in town."

"Where?"

"It's on the other end of town," Star explained. "Near to where all the rich people live. It's the first place they see when they come down the hills."

"Who told you about it?"

"I heard someone talking about it at the market. He has a big collection all ready to go."

"Why are you worried? People love your art."

"They didn't really have a choice all this time," Star grumbled. "My gallery was the only place you could get paintings of the region."

"And now you have competition," Jenny summed up.

"More importantly, the buyers have a choice," Star said.

Her fear and uncertainty were written clearly on her face.

"What if they don't like my stuff anymore?"

"I don't think that's possible," Jenny said loyally. "How long have you been doing this? Thirty years, forty? You are a pro at this. It's evident in your work."

"Art is subjective," Star pointed out. "What if people like his work more than mine?"

"You said it yourself," Jenny smiled. "Some people might like this new guy's paintings and some will like yours. Tourist trade is picking up in Pelican Cove. And most people roam around on Main Street. Anyone walking on the boardwalk or the beach can see your art gallery. They can't help but walk in."

"You think so?" Star asked.

"I know so. And we have your website set up too. You have more orders than you can fill right now. I don't see why you are getting so worked up."

"I have always been the only artist on the island," Star muttered.

"Have you met this guy yet?" Jenny asked. "What's his name, anyway?"

"Frank something," Star said. "He's not from around here. I can't understand why he came to Pelican Cove."

"Go meet him," Jenny suggested. "Introduce yourself."

"He could be a recluse," Star mused.

"So? He'll turn you away. But you will have tried."

"I think that's a good idea. Can I take some of these cupcakes with me?"

"That's a great idea," Jenny said brightly. "He's going to like you, don't worry. Everyone does."

Star could be outspoken but she was always ready to lend a helping hand. Although she wasn't born in Pelican Cove, she had endeared herself to the locals. After forty odd years on the island, she was almost a native.

"I guess I can finally talk shop with someone," Star said eagerly.

"That's the right attitude," Jenny cheered. "You'll be fine."

Jenny pulled out one of the fancy boxes they had recently ordered. With more and more people wanting to carry Jenny's sweet treats away with them, Petunia had suggested they print some fancy boxes with the Boardwalk Café's logo on them. Jenny packed four cupcakes in the box and tied it with a satin ribbon.

"Does he have any family?" she asked. "Will these be enough?"

"I don't know," Star shrugged. "I guess I'll find out."

Star took the box and went out. Jenny hoped she would hit it off with the new artist.

The phone rang. It was Betty Sue. Jenny was almost done with her day's chores. She rushed to the Bayview

Inn to see what was wrong with Heather. The next hour was spent consoling Heather and letting her cry on her shoulder. Jenny didn't think it was the right time to tell Heather about Gianni's wife.

"How long is she going to mope around like this?" Betty Sue said worriedly.

She was twisting her lace handkerchief in her hands. Her hands were never still, even when she wasn't knitting.

"We have to give her time, Betty Sue," Jenny sighed. "Grief is personal, I guess. We can't predict how long she will take to get over Gianni."

"I hate that man," Betty Sue spat. "He misled my Heather when he was alive, and now he's messing with her even after he's dead."

Jenny fully agreed with Betty Sue.

"Why don't you find some dirt on him? I'm sure he wasn't a good man."

Jenny debated how much she wanted to reveal to Betty Sue.

"I'm working on it," she nodded. "Although I'm not sure if it will make a difference. Gianni has become some kind of hero in Heather's eyes."

Betty Sue surprised Jenny by what she said next.

"Heather needs to go out on a date. Why don't you fix up something for her on that Internet?"

"She has to be ready to meet other people, Betty Sue. Don't worry, just give it some time."

"You need to get some dirt on that man, and soon," Betty Sue insisted.

"I did find out something," Jenny finally admitted. "I spoke to his wife today."

Betty Sue sucked in a breath.

"Keep digging, Jenny. Make my Heather smile again."

Jenny went to the seafood market to shop for dinner. Chris met her as soon as she entered.

"The catch just came in," he told her. "I put aside all your favorites for you."

Back home, Jenny drew a bath for herself. She lit some scented candles and poured herself some lemonade. The hot water soothed her and she dozed a bit in the big clawfoot tub. The renovators had suggested installing a jetted tub in the lavish bathroom but Jenny had opted against it.

She dressed in her favorite faded jeans and an old

sweatshirt and hopped down to the kitchen. There was some warmth in the air but she craved something rich and comforting. She slid a bread pudding in the oven and made her special whiskey and butter sauce to go on top. Then she made a simple sauce with olives and cherry tomatoes to go with the fish.

Star regaled them with an account of her encounter with the new artist.

"He didn't say much, but his eyes gleamed when he saw the cupcakes."

"Nobody can resist those cupcakes," Adam said lovingly, placing his hand over Jenny's.

"You have nothing to worry about, babe," Jimmy told Star loyally.

Jenny yearned to go for a walk. Adam and Jimmy loaded the dishwasher and helped clear up. Tank came over with his leash in his mouth and dropped it at Jenny's feet.

Jenny clipped the leash on and hugged Tank.

"Are you coming?" she asked Adam.

Tank strained on his leash, almost dragging her to the door.

The salty breeze and the flowers from the garden

perfumed the air with a peculiar fragrance. Jenny closed her eyes and took a deep breath. A familiar arm came around her shoulders and she snuggled close to Adam.

They walked away from the house, Jenny throwing a ball for Tank.

"The contractor called today," Adam told Jenny. "They are almost done at my house. I should be able to move back soon."

"Do you have to go?"

"I've imposed on you long enough."

"Don't say that," Jenny argued. "I've enjoyed having you here at Seaview. The house is big enough."

"So is your heart," Adam crooned in her ear.

He planted a kiss on her head and stared into her eyes.

"I enjoyed these past few months, Jenny. We have been living in a dream."

"And I don't want to wake up from it," Jenny nodded.

"There are things to consider," Adam said cryptically.

Adam's twin girls were at college. They came home periodically. Jenny had welcomed them at Seaview but she guessed they missed their own home.

"Have the twins said something?"

"The twins have said a lot," Adam smiled. "I think I agree with them."

Jenny blushed at the suggestion. They had never discussed the status of their relationship. Jenny maintained Adam was her friend and a guest in her house. And yes, they were dating. What was the next step in their relationship?

"Tank and I are going to miss you."

"You'll still come here for your walk, won't you?" Jenny asked with a pout.

Months ago, she had run into Adam and Tank while walking on the beach. They had struck up a conversation and continued meeting with tacit agreement.

"We will try, but we may not make it out here every night."

"Then stay," Jenny urged. "Don't go yet."

Adam knew he needed to move out of Seaview before he could take any next steps. He had a solid plan and he couldn't wait to put it into action.

"We've got a couple of weeks," Adam consoled her. "But I will be gone by Spring Fest."

"Is something special happening then?"

"Wait and see," Adam grinned. "Now, did someone mention dessert?"

"Don't change the subject," Jenny said, glaring at him with her hands on her hips.

They had reached the patio at the back of the house. Star and Jimmy sat outside, enjoying their bread pudding. Adam pulled out a chair for Jenny.

"Adam's moving out," Jenny told her aunt. "It's going to be just the two of us again."

Chapter 5

Jenny brewed a fresh pot of coffee and wondered how to tackle Heather. Lately, Heather had the tendency of bursting into tears at the slightest provocation. But Jenny wanted to tell Heather about Gianni's wife before she heard about it from somewhere else.

"Can you come here before the others?" Jenny asked Heather over the phone. "We need to talk."

"Whatever," Heather mumbled without an ounce of interest.

She arrived at the café half an hour later, looking like she just got out of bed. Her eyes were sunken and there were circles under her eyes.

"How are you holding up, Heather?" Jenny asked with concern.

"Never mind that," Heather snapped. "Why did you want me here?"

Jenny led Heather to a small table inside the kitchen and made her sit down. Heather declined the offer of a freshly frosted cupcake but grabbed the cup of coffee Jenny poured for her.

"I found something out yesterday," Jenny began. "It

doesn't make any difference now."

"What is it?"

"Promise me you won't flip."

"Spit it out already, Jenny!"

"I was looking Gianni up on the Internet." Jenny didn't know how to break it gently. "He was married, Heather. I am so sorry."

"Not for long," Heather said coolly.

"You knew about it?" Jenny burst out. "You never mentioned it."

"It wasn't a big deal," Heather shrugged. "It was a sham of a marriage. Gianni was going to divorce her pretty soon. His lawyer was drawing up the papers."

Jenny reflected over her conversation with Tiffany, Gianni's wife. Tiffany hadn't been aware of the impending divorce.

"Why was he leaving her?"

"She cheated on him," Heather drawled. "Gianni wasn't too happy with that."

Jenny stifled a laugh. It was the pot calling the kettle black.

"Who would be?" she said lamely. "Does she know about you?"

"I don't know," Heather shrugged. "Like you said, it doesn't matter now. What's with all the questions, Jenny?"

The Magnolias came in one by one and Heather went back to sulking in a corner.

Jenny went to The Steakhouse on her way back home. She had left her scarf in the restaurant the last time she was there. The hostess had told her to come and look in their Lost and Found. It was a pricey scarf with a designer label, a remnant of Jenny's old life. She admitted she still had some pleasant memories attached to it though and she didn't want to lose it.

It was an hour before the restaurant opened for dinner. The staff was setting the tables, filling salt shakers and getting the place ready. An attractive young woman Jenny recognized led her to a small office. Jenny spotted her scarf right away.

"Oh good," she exclaimed. "I didn't want to lose it."

"Did you have a good time here?" the girl asked eagerly. "It wasn't our best night."

"I was here Valentine's weekend," Jenny said. "I loved how you decorated the place. It was romantic."

"We try to do our best," the girl said solicitously. "I was referring to that other girl from your party. The one with the older man."

"Heather?"

The girl nodded. "She got into a big fight. You didn't know?"

Jenny shook her head. She had no idea what the girl was talking about.

"There was this other woman, platinum blonde, very attractive," the girl went on. "She was obviously a tourist. She got a table behind yours."

"Go on," Jenny urged.

"Heather got into an argument with her in the restroom. The woman pushed Heather. Heather pushed her back and slapped her. The woman fell and broke a heel. There was quite a ruckus."

Jenny was staring at the girl with wide eyes.

"We didn't hear any of that!"

"Well, the music was loud, I guess," the girl mused. "And we broke up the fight. A couple of the guys helped."

"Heather was gone from the table for some time,"

Jenny recollected. "I do remember that now. I thought she was fixing her face."

Jenny blushed as she remembered that night. She had been busy holding hands with Adam, thinking of the surprise she had planned for him when they got home. She had barely spared a glance at Heather.

"Heather's much older than me, of course," the girl prattled on. "But I've seen her around with that cute poodle. I never thought she was capable of using her fists."

"Any idea what they were fighting about?"

The girl looked uncomfortable.

"The blonde called Heather a slut."

Jenny had a good idea who the woman must have been. She thanked the girl for the scarf and walked home, lost in thought.

Why was Heather being so secretive? She had kept things from Jenny and also lied to her blatantly. Jenny didn't recognize the person Heather was turning into.

Star was pacing the floor in the great room at Seaview, rubbing her hands.

"What's the matter?" Jenny asked.

"I did something impulsive. I asked that new artist over for dinner."

"That's wonderful," Jenny assured her. "It will give you a chance to get to know him. We can get him talking and find out what his intentions are."

"Do we have enough food?" Star asked. "We don't have fish today."

"You don't worry about a thing. Let me handle everything."

Jenny called Jason and invited him for dinner.

"I need your discerning eye," she laughed over the phone. "We have a special guest."

Jason had just finished wrapping up a case. He agreed to pick up some shrimp from the seafood market.

Jenny marinated chicken breasts in garlic and balsamic vinegar. She plucked rosemary from the garden and crushed it before adding it to the marinade. She would make her special wine sauce to go with it.

Jason arrived a few minutes before the artist. He put on an apron and started chopping salad.

"Where's that grouchy house guest of yours?" he asked with a wink.

"Adam's working late. He won't be home for dinner."

"So I'm a sit in for him?"

Jenny placed her hands on her hips and glared at Jason.

"No good deed goes unpunished, huh. Here I thought you would enjoy a home cooked meal. But I guess I was wrong."

They bantered for a while, comfortable in each other's company. Jenny asked after Kandy but she was secretly glad the slightly overbearing lawyer wasn't with them.

The doorbell rang and they heard Star welcome someone.

"Frank's here," she said as she led a short, stout man in.

Star towered over him, at least a foot taller. The man had long arms and the slender fingers of an artist. His face was pockmarked and he wore his white hair in a crew cut.

"Frank Lopez," he introduced himself.

Jimmy Parsons hovered close to Star, his eyes keenly observing the newcomer.

Jenny brought out her crab dip and Jason poured wine. Frank declined.

"I don't drink," he said, looking at Jimmy's lemonade. "I'll have the same."

"Where are you from, Frank?" Jenny asked.

"I lived in the southwest most of my life," the artist replied. "I guess I got tired of painting canyons and deserts."

There was some polite laughter at that.

"I sold my house, put all my stuff in an Airstream and set off one day."

"Doesn't get simpler than that," Star agreed.

Jenny sensed a longing in her aunt's voice. Her aunt had been a hippie in her younger days. Jenny wondered if she still dreamt of hitting the road.

"How's that working out for you?" Jason asked.

"Much better than I ever imagined," Frank said enthusiastically. "I stop where I want, set up my easel and start painting. It's been great for my art."

"What brings you to Pelican Cove?" Jimmy asked. "Very few westerners venture into our neck of the woods."

"I was in Vermont last fall," Frank explained. "I ran into a family who hailed from the Eastern Shore. They told me so much about the region. I decided I was going to spend the next summer here."

"Wasn't Maine closer to where you were?" Jimmy asked curiously. "It's not a bad spot to paint."

"I was there last summer," Frank laughed. "Painted the cliffs and the mountains ad nauseum. The beaches here are different."

"No place is quite like Pelican Cove," Star said fondly. "Most of the beauty here is untouched. We have our share of tourists, but we are not very commercialized."

"I confess I'm something of a gourmand," Frank said, piercing his fork into a plump shrimp.

Jenny had served dinner and the lively conversation had moved to the dinner table.

Frank complimented Jenny's cooking.

"I'm making it a point to taste local delicacies. The Chesapeake crabs and oysters are next on my list."

"You came to the right place for that," Jenny told him. "Wait till you taste our soft shell crabs."

"I'm also big on meditation," Frank went on. "It helps my art, you know. Peace of mind is underrated."

"I hear you are setting up a gallery?" Star asked, finally

broaching the topic that was bothering her.

Frank nodded. "It's temporary. I have landscapes from all over the country. A lot of water colors."

"I mostly use oil on canvas," Star told him.

Jenny served a cheesecake for dessert. Frank went home with a big smile on his face.

"He seems okay," Jenny said. "He'll be gone before fall sets in, Star. You don't have anything to worry about."

Jimmy wasn't too taken with the newcomer.

"I don't buy it," he said. "Peace of mind, my ass."

"You promised not to swear, Jimmy," Star chided him.

Jenny went out to see Jason off. He thanked her for the lovely dinner.

"Are you Heather's lawyer?" Jenny asked him.

Jason nodded.

"So you don't have to tell me everything she tells you?"

"Anything Heather tells me is confidential, Jenny. You know that."

"She's been lying to me, Jason. She knew Gianni was married but she never told us about it."

"Maybe she didn't want you to judge her."

"I can believe that," Jenny said. "But get this. She picked a fight with Gianni's wife at The Steakhouse. What was Gianni's wife doing there? And why was Heather punching her lights out?"

"I'll talk to her about it," Jason promised.

Jenny kept thinking about Heather as she tossed and turned that night.

"What else are you hiding, Heather?" she demanded the next morning.

Heather's eyes were swollen with too much sleep.

"Get off my back, Jenny," Heather snarled.

"I know you punched Gianni's wife. That's not like you."

Heather shrugged.

"What did you do after you went home with Gianni?" Jenny pressed. "You need to come clean if you want me to help you."

"I don't need your help," Heather wailed. "I'm innocent."

"So tell me what you did."

"I must have gone home," Heather said with a frown. "I woke up in my own bed."

"When did you go home?" Jenny pressed. "And how?"

Heather clutched her forehead in her hands as she sat down.

"Leave me alone, Jenny. I don't owe you any explanations."

"You can blow me off all you want, Heather," Jenny said, shaking her head. "But you can't stop the questions. The police will keep asking them and you better have an answer for them."

"I don't remember, okay?" Heather cried. "I went home with Gianni. I think we had a drink."

"You were already drunk."

"So what?" Heather scowled. "I woke up in my own bed the next day. I don't know how I got there. You can ask me the same question a dozen times but my answer will be the same. I don't know."

Jenny balled her fists as she realized how hopeless the situation was.

"I think you're in trouble, sweetie," Jenny said softly. "God help you get out of this."

Chapter 6

"Are you sure she won't be mad at us?" Molly asked timidly.

Jenny and Molly were driving out of town in Jenny's car, headed to the small town in Delaware where Gianni's wife lived. Jenny had wisely decided against taking Heather with them. Normally, the three friends always went out of town together, but this time they had slipped out without telling Heather about their plans.

"Given the way she's acting lately, I am sure she'll throw a fit," Jenny said with a grimace. "Let her. We are doing this for her own good."

"I don't feel so good about it," Molly whined.

Heather had taken the slightest opportunity to belittle Molly since she got together with Chris. Jenny knew her concerns were justified.

"I'll handle her, don't worry."

They drove for over an hour and Jenny crossed the state border. The town they entered seemed to be smaller than Pelican Cove.

"This place looks deserted," Jenny observed. "Hard to

imagine a doctor having a thriving practice here."

"Gianni set up shop in Pelican Cove," Molly reminded her. "Maybe he had a clinic in a whole bunch of small towns up and down the coast."

"Hold that thought," Jenny said as an attractive platinum blonde pulled up in a Mercedes convertible.

Jenny waited as the girl tottered on her heels and went inside the rundown diner. Her chiseled face hinted at Botox and her flawless complexion had probably seen some chemical peels. Jenny switched off her car and stepped out.

The girls followed the other woman into the diner. She had bagged one of the three booths inside. The faux red leather was peeling and there was a smell of burnt cheese in the air.

"You must be Tiffany," Jenny said, taking a seat opposite the woman. "Thanks for coming to meet us."

The girls introduced themselves. Tiffany Costa was friendly enough. She laughed openly and asked the girls how they knew her husband.

Jenny hesitated before replying.

"Gianni knew a friend of ours. Actually, he was dating her for the past few months."

"You're talking about Heather," Tiffany said, fiddling with the sugar sachets on the table.

A tired, grumpy looking waitress came and poured coffee. Jenny took one look at the murky brown liquid and pushed her mug away.

"Do you prefer tea?" the waitress asked her with a smirk. "I've got tea bags."

"You knew Heather?" Molly asked incredulously.

Jenny hadn't told her about the infamous fight at The Steakhouse.

"I saw their photos," Tiffany said wearily. "The whole world saw them, of course. He brought her home once."

Jenny wondered what kind of a cad Gianni had been.

"That must have been hard."

"Gianni had a thing for younger women," Tiffany said. "Younger, beautiful women. He dated them for a while and promised to marry them."

"And?" Molly asked, holding her breath.

"He dumped them when he found someone new."

Tiffany shrugged and took a sip of the coffee. She

seemed pretty cool about the whole thing.

"You were fine with all that?" Jenny pressed.

"He always came back to me," Tiffany told them. "So when he was in the mood for these indiscretions, I just looked the other way."

"I'm guessing the lifestyle didn't hurt."

"I made my choice," Tiffany said coldly. "I'm allowed to do that."

Tiffany seemed to get a bit defensive after that.

"Can you tell us anything else about Gianni?" Molly asked.

"What do you want to know?"

"Why did you live in this town, for instance?" Jenny asked. "There must be hardly any patients here."

"This place was just right for Gianni," Tiffany said cryptically.

"How so?"

"Gianni preyed on older people," Tiffany said with a sigh. "People who were not all there," she said, tapping her forehead with a finger. "He fleeced them as much as he could."

"Are you saying he was dishonest?" Molly asked in shock.

"He was a master at duping people," Tiffany said, her eyes gleaming. "He chose small isolated towns where most of the people were senior citizens. They were alone or their kids lived in some city. Either way, they didn't have anyone looking after them."

"What was he doing in Pelican Cove?" Jenny asked, aghast.

"He was done here. Pelican Cove was next on his list. He already had a nice racket going there."

"Why didn't you live there with him?"

"I did," Tiffany said with a shrug. "Off and on."

"Funny we never ran into you," Jenny said, narrowing her eyes.

Most new people in town came to the Boardwalk Café for a meal. Jenny was sure Tiffany had never visited the café.

"That was all part of Gianni's plan," Tiffany explained. "I was keeping a low profile."

"I don't understand," Jenny said coldly.

"He was wooing Heather, right?" Tiffany said with a

yawn. "According to Gianni, it was easy to befriend people as a single man. He always showered attention on one of the local girls. That allowed him to get a foot in, meet the movers and shakers in town."

"How smart of him," Jenny said sarcastically.

"He was sneaky that way," Tiffany agreed.

"I don't understand," Jenny said, sitting up. "If you already knew Heather, what was the fight about?"

"You heard about that?" Tiffany asked with a laugh. "I was just acting on Gianni's instructions."

"Kindly explain …" Jenny said with a roll of her eyes.

"Heather was getting clingy. She probably expected some kind of grand gesture for Valentine's weekend. That's why Gianni invited me there."

"What were you going to do?"

"I just had to show up at that dingy restaurant and tell Heather I was meeting Gianni later."

"I guess she didn't believe you."

Tiffany shook her head, rubbing a spot on her chin. It seemed like she was remembering the fight.

"That girl's got a mean right hook," she said with a

shudder. "She told me she was the one going home with Gianni. She warned me to stay away."

"Did you?" Jenny asked.

"I was just supposed to plant a seed of doubt. I got that done."

Jenny peered at Tiffany's face, trying to gauge if she was telling the truth.

"You are sure you didn't go home and lie in wait for Gianni?"

"Gianni was a mean drunk," Tiffany said. "I didn't want to be anywhere near him that night."

"Would you say Gianni was depressed about something?" Jenny asked as a last resort.

The police hadn't mentioned the possibility of suicide but she wanted to rule it out.

"Honey, Gianni made other people cry. He was happier than a pig in mud!"

Jenny thanked Tiffany for meeting them.

"Sure. Call me anytime."

She breezed out of the diner ahead of them. Jenny belatedly realized Tiffany looked nothing like a grieving widow.

"Heather had a close call," Molly said on the way back.

"You don't believe she was okay with Gianni being married?" Jenny asked her.

"He must have convinced her he was going to leave his wife," Molly shrugged.

"Heather must have lost it when she saw Tiffany at the restaurant," Jenny observed.

Had Heather been angry enough to take revenge?

Jenny and Molly were both hungry by the time they got back in town.

"Petunia must be closing up, but I can rustle up something for us to eat," Jenny promised.

They were surprised to see a group of women arguing loudly at the café.

"We have to do something about this," Barb Norton said, slapping the table. "It's your duty to support us, Betty Sue."

"What's going on?" Jenny asked her aunt.

Petunia, Star and Betty Sue sat on one side of the table. Barb Norton sat on the other side, glaring at them like a judge. Heather was nowhere to be seen.

"Just wait and watch," Star whispered.

Jenny pulled out a bowl of chicken salad and scooped it generously over two large slices of artisan bread. She added sliced tomatoes and lettuce and squirted her honey mustard dressing on top. She cut the sandwich in two pieces and put them on a plate.

Molly and Jenny munched their sandwich as they listened to Barb and Betty Sue.

Betty Sue's needles clacked as she went on knitting, refusing to look up.

"Are you paying attention, Betty Sue?" Barb roared. "We need to go talk to those Newburys."

Betty Sue finally looked up. She had a weary look in her eyes.

"I don't like talking to John about his business."

"His business is threatening the fabric of our society," Barb said pompously. "It's everyone's business now."

"Why don't you go the usual route? Form a committee?" Betty Sue clucked. "We can then draw up some kind of proposal and take it to the Newburys."

"I am doing all that," Barb said sternly. "But we need

to push things forward. I say we take a delegation up there right now."

Star giggled at the mention of a delegation. Barb breathed fire on her.

"Is this about the medical dispensary?" Jenny mumbled, chewing on her delicious sandwich.

"Don't talk with your mouth full, young lady!" Barb snapped. "We are talking about the drug farms."

"Same difference," Jenny muttered.

"Are you saying you support this heinous undertaking?" Barb scowled at her. "I was counting on you, Jenny."

"My mind's not made up either way," Jenny said, wiping her mouth with a paper napkin. "I need more information."

"I agree with Jenny," Molly said softly.

"You too?" Barb pounced on Molly. "Have you forgotten what we did to save your job?"

"I am grateful for what the town did for me, Barb," Molly spoke up. "But this is a different issue."

"Stop blabbering," Betty Sue commanded. "You are giving me a headache."

"Put that knitting down, Betty Sue, and come with me," Barb pressed. "We should all go."

"You know Ada doesn't see people without an appointment," Betty Sue pleaded.

Ada Newbury never let anyone forget that she was the richest woman in town. She looked down her nose at everyone and was a trial to be around.

Barb and Betty Sue argued a bit more and Betty Sue finally gave in. They all set off in two cars, Jenny looking forward to seeing someone take Ada down a peg or two.

The guard at the gate let them in when he spied Betty Sue in Jenny's back seat. Ada kept them waiting for half an hour before she emerged, dressed to the nines.

"Ladies," she said with her nose in the air. "Is it an emergency? I am getting late for a party."

"Sit down, Ada," Barb Norton said brusquely. "We have come to talk about this drug farm of yours."

"My husband handles the business," Ada snipped. "People generally take an appointment and meet him in his office."

"Your husband has gone too far this time," Barb quipped. "We need you to bring him to his senses."

"Be very careful what you say next, Barb," Ada said angrily. "Don't forget you are sitting in my parlor."

"We love our town, Ada," Barb said. "It's rustic but simple and we manage it as well as possible with the limited resources we have."

Ada reminded them she donated liberally to those resources.

"The town has always been grateful for your largesse," Barb said firmly. "But we cannot open our doors to a drug business."

"I think there is some misunderstanding," Ada clucked. "We are planning to open a dispensary that will treat people."

"A marijuana dispensary?" Barb said hoarsely. "Over my dead body!"

"Stop being so dramatic," Ada said in a bored voice.

The conversation derailed after that. Ada clapped her hands and a couple of maids ran into the room. She ordered them to escort the women out.

"Now what?" Jenny asked as they stood outside the Boardwalk Café.

"We march on," Barb said, plunging her fist in the air. "Say no to cannabis!" she yelled. "Say no to drugs!"

Chapter 7

Jenny sat in Jason's office, moodily sipping from a bottle of juice. Jason leaned back in his chair with his hands behind his head, staring at a corner.

"Are you sure about this, Jenny?"

"I only have Tiffany's word for it, but why would she lie?"

"I can think of a number of reasons. She says Gianni told her about the girls he dated. But we only have her word for it."

"Any other wife would have been shocked."

"We don't know if she was really okay with all this," Jason warned. "All I am saying is, take anything she says with a pinch of salt. You just met the woman."

Jenny didn't like to be called gullible. She thought she had a good eye for people.

"What about the other stuff she said?"

"That's also her word against his."

"So you don't think he was shady? Any man who can cheat on his wife and sweet talk a young girl into going around with him …"

"We all know what he did with Heather," Jason said, warding her off. "But medical fraud …"

Jason went back to staring in the distance.

"We can't just sit around talking about this," Jenny said. "Let's go out and do something."

"Like what? Raid Gianni's office?"

Jenny's eyes gleamed and a smile lit up her face.

"Who's going to stop us?"

"I'm a lawyer, Jenny. I can't just go breaking and entering."

"We may not have to," Jenny said, springing to her feet.

She almost dragged Jason along with her.

Gianni Costa lived in a ranch style house a few blocks off Main Street. There was another ranch adjoining his which had served as his clinic. The shingle hanging off a pole announced it as the family practice of Dr. Gianni Costa, MD. Jenny walked up to the door and turned the handle. The door opened easily.

"Viola!" she said to Jason. "We are not breaking any

laws going through an open door."

"I guess not," Jason shrugged.

Jenny rushed through the waiting room at the front and entered a door marked 'Staff only'.

"He must have kept some records," she mumbled to herself.

Gianni turned out to be a meticulous record keeper. Jenny spotted files in a drawer and started rifling through them.

"What are you looking for, exactly?" Jason asked.

"Anything out of the ordinary," Jenny quipped. "Heather was a patient?" she murmured as she pulled out a thick file.

Her mouth was hanging open two minutes later.

"Look at what this says," she said, pulling at Jason's sleeve. "According to this, Heather was Gianni's patient and visited him every day of the week."

"She visited him alright," Jason sniggered.

"Can you be serious for a minute?" Jenny taunted. "It's all written here. Heather Morse is a patient. There are prescription records too."

Jenny slumped into a chair, looking worried.

"Is Heather sick?" she exclaimed. "Does she have some terrible illness she's hiding from everyone?"

"You're being dramatic, Jenny," Jason said lightly. "She might have had some minor complaint."

"This says she had an appointment every day. There is some kind of code under diagnosis but I don't know what that means."

"Let's go talk to Heather."

Jason sounded resigned. He knew Jenny wouldn't rest until she got to the bottom of this.

Jenny called Heather from the clinic and asked her to wait at home. She started for the Bayview Inn with Jason.

Betty Sue fussed over them when they got to the inn, plying them with hot tea and cookies.

"Why don't you take a nap, Grandma," Heather suggested. "I've got things under control here."

"You're just trying to get rid of me," Betty Sue glowered.

Jenny sighed with relief when she went up the stairs to her room.

"What have you been hiding, Heather?" she asked, turning to look at her friend. "Please tell me nothing's wrong with you."

"What do you mean, Jenny?"

Heather looked bewildered as Jenny narrated what she had seen.

"I never saw Gianni professionally," Heather said firmly. "There must be some mistake."

"As far as I know, there's only one Heather Morse in Pelican Cove," Jenny said stoutly. "Something is fishy here."

"I still go to old Dr. Smith," Heather said again. "He's treated me since I came to live with Grandma."

"So Tiffany was right," Jenny said to Jason, slapping her leg. "That Gianni was doing something illegal."

"When did you talk to Tiffany?" Heather asked, springing to her feet. "She had it in for Gianni."

"I don't care what her relationship was with Gianni," Jenny dismissed. "She told us Gianni cheated his patients. I am beginning to think she was right."

"Just because Gianni's not here to defend himself …"

Heather curled her fists and looked anguished. Her

eyes filled with tears.

"Get hold of yourself, Heather," Jenny said, grabbing her by the shoulders and shaking her. "Gianni's gone, and I say you are well rid of him."

"He was a good man," Heather blubbered through her tears.

"He was a nasty crook who was just taking you for a ride," Jenny said mercilessly. "I'm going to prove it to you."

Jenny stomped out of the Bayview Inn, muttering to herself.

"Can you give me a ride home?" she requested Jason. "I have to get ready for dinner. We are going on a double date with Molly and Chris."

"We could have triple dated," Jason said in a hurt tone.

Jenny didn't think she could tolerate another evening with Kandy the lawyer.

"Some other time," she said glibly.

Jenny took a quick shower and agonized over what to wear. She tried on and discarded four dresses. Finally, she settled on a sunflower yellow dress with a cowl neck. She rubbed the heart shaped charm around her neck as she gazed at herself in the mirror. The phone rang just then and Jenny's face lit up when she saw it was her son. She pressed the video button. She needed to see her beloved Nicky.

"When are you getting home, scamp?" she asked lovingly. "A little bird told me you are spending spring break in Pelican Cove."

"No way, Mom," Nick groaned. "You know I am going to Cancun with my friends."

They chatted for a while and Nick hung up after promising to visit soon. Jenny's face lit up in a thousand watt smile. There was a knock on the door.

Adam stood outside, leaning on his cane. He looked handsome in a black silk shirt. His faded jeans hugged his lean body.

"Ready to roll, Madam?" he grinned.

"Are we picking them up?" Jenny asked Adam as she got into the car.

They were going to an Italian restaurant in a nearby town. The Eastern Shore was home to plenty of small towns like Pelican Cove. The area was paradise for foodies, with eclectic restaurants lining the shore from north to south.

"Chris mentioned some errands," Adam told her. "They will meet us at the restaurant."

"Good," Jenny smiled, placing her hand in Adam's.

Molly and Chris were sipping wine and munching on garlic bread when the hostess ushered Adam and Jenny to their table. Jenny let out a shriek merely seconds after she sat down.

"Is that a ring, Molly?"

Molly's face glowed in the candle light.

Jenny whipped her head toward Chris. He was beaming at Molly. Molly clasped his hand in hers and held it up for Jenny.

"Congratulations, man!" Adam said, slapping Chris on the back.

"It's a promise ring," Chris said, clearing his throat. "Sort of a pre-engagement ring."

"Chris surprised me with the most beautiful engagement ring." Molly sounded hushed. "But I thought we would wear a promise ring first."

"But why?" Jenny wailed. "I can't wait to plan your wedding."

"We are taking it slow," Molly said, looking lovingly at Chris. "There's no rush."

"That's just mumbo jumbo," Adam dismissed. "As far

as I am concerned, congratulations are in order. We need some champagne here."

They poured the bubbly and toasted the happy couple. Molly chattered nonstop over the osso buco, a slow cooked dish of wine braised veal. They had tiramisu for dessert and Jenny ordered an espresso to round off the meal.

"Am I allowed to tell people about this?" Jenny asked Molly.

"I'll tell them tomorrow," Molly said shyly. "I'm so happy, Jenny," she said later as they waited outside for the men to bring their cars around. "I feel like I'm in a dream."

"Chris is a good guy," Jenny assured her. "You couldn't have chosen better."

"I want to be sure he loves me," Molly said with a hint of doubt in her voice. "Technically, I'm his rebound relationship."

"Is that why you went for the promise ring?" Jenny asked her.

Molly nodded. "I want him to be sure. Very sure."

"You're one brave girl, Molly. Anyone in your position would have dragged Chris to the altar."

"I've been there," Molly reminded her, referring to her previous marriage. "You understand, don't you, Jenny? When I tie the knot again, it will be for the last time."

Jenny reflected over how different Molly was from Heather. Molly was timid but level headed. Heather was headstrong and impulsive. Chris had fallen for both these women at one time or another.

Adam accompanied Chris to the other end of the parking lot. It was late and the lot had emptied while they lingered over their meal.

"So you are almost leg-shackled," Adam laughed as he patted Chris on the back. "How does it feel?"

Chris wrung a hand through his hair. The smile he had worn all evening was nowhere to be seen.

"You know what's happening with Heather?" he muttered. "I felt pressured."

"You don't love Molly?" Adam scowled. "Are you messing with her, Chris?"

"I do love her," Chris said uncertainly. "But what if Heather needs me? I promised I would always be there for her."

"Are you kidding me?" Adam snapped at Chris. "You should have thought of that before you slipped on that ring."

He put his hand on Chris's shoulder.

"I think you are getting cold feet. Happens to the best of us."

"But what about Heather?" Chris asked with a frown.

"Heather will be fine," Adam said. "She left you, Chris. You accepted that and moved on. You need to look ahead now. Molly's a good soul. She will make you happy for the rest of your days."

"I do love Molly," Chris said earnestly. "But I feel responsible for Heather."

"Heather will be fine," Adam consoled him. "She's not alone. We will all take care of her."

Adam kept quiet about his conversation with Chris. He knew Jenny would fly off the handle if she learned what was going on in Chris's mind. He said good night to Jenny outside her door and limped to his room in search of pain pills.

Jenny brushed her hair and smiled at herself in the mirror. She was happy for Molly and Chris. Chris had always impressed her as a level headed young guy. He would take care of her friend. Her brows furrowed in concern as her phone trilled suddenly. It was past midnight. Her heart thudded in her chest as she thought of her son. She hoped he was fine.

Jenny checked the caller id and crossed her fingers before answering the phone.

"Jason? Is something wrong? Why are you calling so late?"

Jason's voice was heavy with emotion.

"Kandy dumped me."

"What?" Jenny exclaimed. "When?"

"She just sent me an email," Jason said grimly. "She doesn't want to see me anymore."

Chapter 8

Jason refused to speak about Kandy the next day.

"I bet she's just pulling your leg."

"Let's not talk about this, Jenny."

Jenny didn't know what to say. Kandy hadn't seemed like the kind who would settle down, especially in a small, isolated town like Pelican Cove. She had a high flying career in the city. Jenny had been surprised she stuck to Jason all those months.

"Did she give a reason?" Jenny had asked Jason the previous night.

"None," he had lamented. "It just says our lives don't align any more. What does that even mean?"

Jason was putting on a stoic face that morning. Her anguished and hurt friend from the previous night was nowhere in evidence.

"She'll come around," Jenny said again, giving Jason a hug. "If she doesn't, it's her loss."

"What brings you here, Jenny?" Jason asked with a sigh. "Are you just here to console me or do you have something else on your mind?"

"A bit of both," Jenny said grudgingly.

"Shoot. I'm free for the next few hours."

"Do you know the other doctor in town?"

"Old Dr. Smith?" Jason asked. "Sure. I've been seeing him all my life."

"I have an idea."

Dr. Smith's clinic turned out to be a block away from Jenny's home. Jason had called ahead for an appointment. An elderly nurse hugged and kissed Jason.

"Your half yearly appointment is overdue," she scolded.

Dr. Smith was a slim, energetic man in his seventies. Jenny guessed he was a few years older than her aunt. He welcomed Jason with a hug.

"Who's your friend?" he asked with a twinkle in his eye. "Are you finally taking my advice and starting a family?"

Jenny blushed to the roots of her hair. She hastened to explain.

"Oh, you are the young lady the whole town is talking about," the doctor said. "I've tasted most of your goodies. I just haven't had a chance to come into the Boardwalk Café myself. I'm as good as chained to this place."

The small talk went on for a few minutes until Jenny cleared her throat.

Dr. Smith took the hint.

"Look at me ramble on. So what brings you young people here?"

Dr. Smith's face darkened at the mention of Gianni Costa.

"He was a bad one."

Jenny told him about the records in the doctor's office.

"Heather insists she was never his patient. Do you know why he would have a file with her name on it?"

"I can think of a reason or two," Dr. Smith said grimly.

"Would you please look at some of the papers and give them a once over?"

"I have appointments all day," Dr. Smith apologized. "Can you bring the files here?"

"I can get you a few samples," Jenny nodded.

Jason and Jenny went to Gianni's house again. The

door to the clinic portion was locked this time. A fan whirred inside and the radio was playing. Jenny rapped her knuckles on the door.

A tiny, shriveled woman opened the door, her eyes full of fear.

"Do you work here?" Jenny asked.

"I was Dr. Costa's nurse," the woman said.

Jenny realized she should have guessed that from the colorful scrubs the woman was wearing.

"You do know Dr. Costa is gone?" Jason asked.

The nurse shook her head.

"I was out of town on vacation. Did he say when he will be back?"

"We are not sure," Jenny said smoothly. "We are here for some paperwork. He said you would give it to us."

Jason was staring at Jenny with his mouth agape.

The nurse led them into the office they had been in earlier. Jenny got rid of the woman by asking for a glass of water. She pulled out the topmost boxes and began taking pictures of the papers in the files.

"Do you know what you are doing?" Jason hissed.

Jenny held a finger to her lips, asking him to be quiet.

The nurse came back with the water.

"I don't think you are allowed to touch that," she said mildly. "Those records contain confidential information."

"Sorry," Jenny said sweetly. "I thought I would save you some time."

She made up a name and asked for a duplicate report. The nurse spent some time rifling through the files.

"I don't see your name here," she said with a frown.

Jenny sensed the nurse was finally beginning to get irritated.

"Why don't you keep looking for it?" she said. "I'll be back later."

Jason berated her as soon as they got into the car.

"You know what you were doing? Getting information under false pretenses. This will never stand up in a court of law."

"I'm not thinking that far ahead," Jenny dismissed. "I just want to find out what Gianni was up to."

Dr. Smith's office was closed for lunch.

"I've never seen a doctor's office close in the middle of the day," Jenny said.

"This is Pelican Cove," Jason reminded her. "And everyone has to eat."

Jenny's stomach growled just then.

"It's time for lunch," Jason said with a smile. "How about going to Ethan's Crab Shack?"

Jenny smiled approvingly.

"I'd rather not go back to the café. I know I'll put on an apron and start working as soon as I get in there."

Jenny was feeling guilty about leaving Petunia on her own for so long. But her aunt had promised to help out so she could go play detective.

Ethan Hopkins greeted them with a big smile. He was Adam's twin but he couldn't have been more different.

"I've never been here during the day," Jenny said as they found a table by the water.

"What are you in the mood for?" Jason asked. "I am going for the fish and chips."

Jenny chose the grilled seafood salad. Their food arrived in large platters.

"This salad is huge," Jenny said, picking up a fry from Jason's plate.

Jason pushed his plate away after a few bites and lapsed into silence. Jenny let him be.

They made their way back to Dr. Smith's clinic. The old doctor studied all the photos carefully.

"That man was a crook!" he exclaimed. "I want to look at the rest of his files but I am almost certain what's going on here."

"What?" Jason and Jenny asked.

"Healthcare fraud," the doctor said grimly. "I know some of the names here. As far as I know, these people don't have the conditions Costa treated them for."

"So what was he up to?" Jenny asked, fascinated.

"There are fake visits here," Dr. Smith explained. "And false diagnoses."

"Do you know what these letters mean?" Jenny asked, pointing to some gibberish under 'diagnosis'.

"They are diagnosis codes," the doctor explained. "Each group of letters means something specific. Looks like Costa was getting money from the government based on fake data."

"So Heather was never really his patient?"

"Heather and a few others," the doctor nodded. "He's charging for patient visits that never happened. Also for services or procedures I bet he has not performed."

"Could this have harmed his patients?" Jason asked, aghast.

"Hard to say based on this data," Dr. Smith shrugged. "But I wouldn't put it past him."

Jenny thanked the doctor for his time.

"What now?" Jason asked.

"I'm going to talk to Adam," Jenny said stiffly. "Can you drop me off at the police station?"

Nora, the desk clerk, greeted Jenny as soon as she stepped into the station.

"He's not in a good mood," she warned, jerking her head toward Adam's office.

"So what's new?" Jenny said with a roll of her eyes.

Adam's mood was a popular topic of discussion at his place of work. His coworkers tiptoed around him when his temper flared.

Adam sat with his leg propped up on a chair, struggling to unscrew a bottle of pills.

"What do you want?" he snapped, tossing the bottle to Jenny.

She grabbed it and opened it without much effort. She took out two pills and handed them to Adam. Adam downed them with a glass of water and sighed deeply.

"Sit down," he said in a milder tone. "What brings you here, Jenny? I hear you are painting the town red with Jason Stone."

"Hardly," Jenny said with a grimace. "I didn't know you had Ethan spying on me."

"He brought me lunch," Adam said lightly. "You know I was just kidding. So how many laws have you broken today?"

"None that I know of," Jenny said sullenly. "Wait till you hear what I found."

Jenny spoke for the next few minutes. Adam's face was inscrutable as he listened to her.

"When are you going to learn?" he whined when she stopped to take a breath. "You are meddling in police business."

"You mean I am doing their business. Shouldn't you

or your men have found all this out by now?"

Adam had no answer for that.

"Have you even met Tiffany?" Jenny demanded. "I think she's a potential suspect."

"You must be right, of course," Adam said sarcastically.

"You think Heather is guilty, don't you? Why not Tiffany? She was a woman scorned. And she was right here in Pelican Cove on that night. In fact, she was at The Steakhouse."

"Are you sure about that?" Adam asked.

"Yes, I am sure," Jenny bristled. "Just talk to the staff at the restaurant."

"I have to follow certain procedures," Adam droned. "I can't just run around the place talking up anyone I meet."

"What about this healthcare fraud? Don't you think that is important?"

"That's just an allegation," Adam said. "We don't know he was doing anything wrong for sure. We will have to bring in some specialists. And if there is any connection to his old clinic in Delaware, this case is out of my hands."

"What does that mean?" Jenny asked with alarm.

She was worried about Heather.

"Based on what you told me, whatever crimes Gianni committed crossed state lines. That puts the case out of my jurisdiction."

"I have no such restrictions," Jenny said. "I just want to take care of Heather. I'm going to keep digging."

"This healthcare fraud could be dangerous, Jenny," Adam pleaded. "Who knows how many more people are involved. You need to be careful."

"Jason was with me when we went to Gianni's clinic."

"He should have known better," Adam clucked. "Has he lost his mind?"

"He's just being a good friend," Jenny bristled. "Unlike you."

"My hands are tied," Adam said, literally holding his hands up in the air. "You know I can't be partial to you. The whole town knows I'm your house guest."

Jenny tried to calm herself. Adam always got her riled up with his strait laced ideas.

"Is that all you are?" she asked coquettishly.

"Please be careful, Jenny," Adam begged. "I couldn't bear it if something happened to you."

"I can take care of myself," Jenny said, shaking her head. "Don't you think this whole scam business is important? It might lead you to other suspects."

"I never thought of that!" Adam glared at her. "Why don't you leave me alone and let me think about this?"

"I'm leaving," Jenny said, pushing her chair back.

"Want to go out for dinner?" Adam asked. "You must be tired from running around all day."

Jenny smiled reluctantly.

"I don't mind. I was craving something spicy."

Adam made plans to take her to a Mexican restaurant ten miles up the coast.

"Have a nice day, Sheriff!" Jenny said with a wave as she breezed out of Adam's office.

She had stumbled onto her next course of action while talking to Adam.

Chapter 9

Adam and Jenny sat on the patio, sipping wine. Star and Jimmy were watching a movie. It was one of their favorite things to do after dinner. Jenny had been too tired to go for a walk. They had chosen to relax in the garden instead. Tank sat at Jenny's feet, dozing with one eye closed.

Adam looked at the stone fountain in the garden and let out a sigh.

"I have some news for you, Jenny."

"I know you are eager to move back to your house, Adam, but why don't you wait a few weeks more?"

"It's not about that," Adam hesitated.

Jenny peered into his eyes, trying to guess what he was about to say.

"The DNA results are in. There is no more doubt."

"So it was Lily Davis," Jenny said softly. "Or Lily Bennet if you consider her married name."

Adam nodded in the soft moonlight.

"She was here all along, right in her own backyard."

"Do you think she's still around?" Jenny asked with a shiver.

"What nonsense!" Adam dismissed. "We talked about this, Jenny."

"I know, I know … but all those stories about mysterious lights and the house being haunted … maybe Lily was trying to get someone's attention."

"You amaze me," Adam said with a shake of his head. "You are this smart modern woman one instant and the next instant you start talking like some illiterate person."

"I'm just saying …"

"I guess you feel some kind of compulsion to get to the bottom of this," Adam smirked.

"Believe it or not, I do," Jenny said. "I'm going to do everything I can to find out who killed Lily."

"I wish you luck. We don't have too many resources to assign to a case that old, so you might be the only one fighting for Lily."

"I might need your help, Adam."

"Let me know what you need."

"You're not going to yell at me for meddling with

police business?"

"Not this time," Adam promised.

Jenny thought of Lily as she baked a batch of blueberry muffins the next morning. She wasn't looking forward to telling the Magnolias about Lily.

Betty Sue came in, clutching a ball of white wool under her armpit. Her knitting needles poked out of a tote bag. Heather followed her, biting her nails, looking lost in thought.

"Is she still biting her nails?" Betty Sue asked Jenny.

Jenny followed them out to the deck with a tray loaded with coffee and snacks. Star was coming up the steps from the beach.

"Where's Molly?" Petunia wanted to know.

"I'm right here," Molly said cheerily, looking pretty in an apple green dress.

Jenny didn't waste any time bringing the women up to speed. Betty Sue crossed herself and muttered a prayer.

Lily had been her best friend since childhood.

"I never believed she abandoned her family," Betty Sue said.

"You say that now, Grandma!" Heather said with a sneer. "But you were quick to blame her, just like everyone else."

"How was I supposed to know what happened?" Betty Sue cried. "She disappeared overnight."

"You should have known," Heather stressed. "You should have trusted her."

Jenny sensed Heather wasn't just talking about Lily. Heather's recent wild streak had driven a wedge between her and Betty Sue.

Jenny called Adam from the café.

"Did anyone file a missing person report when Lily disappeared?"

"I'll have Nora look into the archives," Adam promised. "Why don't you come here in a few hours?"

"Let's meet for lunch," Jenny suggested.

Adam pointed to a thin file on his desk when Jenny entered his office with a basket on her arm. They made quick work of the crab salad sandwich she had brought. Jenny was eager to see what the file contained. She pushed the box of cupcakes she had brought toward Adam and flipped open the file.

"Three pages?" she exclaimed. "That's all?"

"There was nothing suspicious about her disappearance. I am surprised they even filed a report."

"Lily wasn't a loose character," Jenny mused. "Why did people believe she had a lover?"

"I think the general impression was that she had lost it. She had become so unpredictable that people were ready to believe anything about her."

Jenny read the reports as she discussed different scenarios with Adam.

"This is from Ann Davis," she spoke up suddenly. "Ann says she saw Lily get into a car. What was Ann doing here, Adam?"

Adam shrugged his shoulders as he licked frosting off his lips.

Jenny decided to go to the Bayview Inn to talk to Betty Sue.

"Of course! I forgot Ann was in town at that time," Betty Sue said. "She and Ricky were both here."

"What were they doing here?" Jenny asked.

"Seaview was a house of mourning, remember? When Lily lost her daughter, Ann and her son came to visit."

"Wasn't there a lot of time in between? Like months?"

"It was a different time, dear," Betty Sue said with a faraway look in her eyes. "People came for a visit and stayed on. No one was in a hurry to rush back anywhere. And Ann and her son, they were family. Seaview was as much their home as Lily's."

"Ann was the one who saw Lily get into that car," Jenny told Betty Sue. "So either Lily really got into a car and came back, or Ann is lying."

"Did I tell you Lily wanted to sell the house?" Betty Sue asked.

"What? No, you never mentioned that."

"Lily began to hate the place after her girl died. She wanted to get away from this place. She might have put an ad in the paper."

"How did Ann feel about it?"

"You will have to ask her," Betty Sue said.

"That's right," Jenny said, her eyes growing wide. "I have Ann's number. I can talk to her. Why didn't I think of that!"

Jenny hurried home later, determined to call Ann Davis. Jenny had bought her house from her. The woman was in her eighties and lived in Texas. Jenny had met her when she came to Pelican Cove a few months ago.

Ann was surprised to hear from Jenny.

"I miss the beach and your café," she told Jenny. "Ricky and I are thinking of visiting again this summer."

"This is your home," Jenny told her. "You are always welcome here."

Ann asked after all the Magnolias. Jenny finally got to the point.

"I was looking at an old police report," she began. "You told the police that you saw Lily get into a car with someone."

"That's right," Ann said in a strong voice. "Got into a dark sedan late at night and never came back. It was a new moon, and the garden was pitch dark. But I saw it all from my window."

"Did you see who was driving?" Jenny pressed. "Do you remember anything else about the car?"

"I wish I did," Ann sighed. "It might have helped the police find Lily. But I guess she never wanted to come back."

"Didn't the police call you?" Jenny asked.

She told Ann about the DNA results.

"I can't believe it," Ann said, suddenly sounding old. "Poor Lily."

"Did you hear a car again that night?" Lily asked. "Or did you hear any noise in the garden?"

She didn't want to spell out her theory. If someone had come back and dug a pit in the garden, surely Ann would have heard something?

"I had a migraine," Ann told Jenny, dashing her hopes. "I took a sleeping pill and went to bed."

"Did you notice anything odd in the garden in the next day or two?"

"I sprained my ankle on the stairs the next day," Ann told her. "I had to keep it elevated for a week."

Jenny told Ann to call her back if she remembered anything new. She hung up, feeling dejected.

She tried to clear her mind as she made dinner. She went out in the garden and stood staring at the fountain, the spot where they had dug up the skeleton. Give me a clue, Lily, she urged silently. Give me something. She plucked a bunch of dill and went inside.

Jenny poured her orange dill marinade over a pan of fish and slid it in the oven.

"Any luck?" Star asked her as they ate dinner.

Jenny shook her head.

"Everything hinges on Ann's testimony. And Ann insists she saw Lily get into that car. If she's lying, I need a way to prove it."

"Didn't we have a toll booth at the bridge in those days?" Star asked Jimmy.

"That's right," Jimmy nodded. "Kids from the high school worked there most times."

Adam slammed his fork down in his plate and swore suddenly.

"I worked there for a few weeks. How could I not remember?"

"It's okay," Jenny teased. "Memory's the first to go when you're getting old."

"You don't get it, Jenny," Adam said urgently. "The purpose behind that booth was to find out how many tourists came to Pelican Cove. The kid working the booth had to note down the tags of all the cars that came and left."

"And your point is?"

"We can check how many cars crossed the bridge to

go out of town that night."

"They keep records from 1991?" Jenny asked doubtfully.

"I'm going to find out," Adam promised.

Jenny greeted Captain Charlie, her favorite customer, the next morning. He was always first in line when the Boardwalk Café opened at 6 AM.

"Here's your muffin, Captain Charlie," Jenny said, handing him a paper bag and a tall cup of coffee. "What do you think about the new dispensary that's opening up in town?"

"I already signed the paper," he told her. "I know they say those pot brownies help with aches and pains, but I ain't going against the town. No Sir."

"What paper?"

"Heather's going around town with it. She'll get around to you soon enough."

Heather came in earlier than usual, holding a clipboard.

"Barb put me to work," she told Jenny. "This is some kind of appeal. It says you're against the marijuana dispensary. Just print your name here and sign next to it."

"You really think it's that bad?"

"I don't think," Heather said, stressing the word think. "When Barb says you have to do something, people generally fall in line."

"I'm not convinced this dispensary is such a bad idea," Jenny argued. "What about all the people it's going to help?"

"Barb says it will harm more people than it will help. Anyway, you can talk about all that at the town hall meeting. Just sign here for now."

"What is Barb going to do with these signatures?"

Heather shrugged.

"I guess she's going to stop the Newburys from getting the licenses they need."

"That sounds vindictive."

"Suit yourself," Heather said. "But get ready to tackle Barb Norton."

Jenny stirred a pot of soup and motioned Heather to sit down. She slid a freshly baked cupcake with pretty pink frosting in front of Heather.

"Lemon with a raspberry filling. Try it."

"I've gained ten pounds since you came into town, Jenny."

"You look as pretty as ever, sweetie."

Jenny patted Heather on her cheek.

"Are Chris and Molly engaged?" Heather asked with a heavy voice. "Why haven't they told me?"

"They are not officially engaged," Jenny explained. "They are somewhere in between." She hesitated before saying anything more. "You know that day is coming though, Heather."

"I've been doing some thinking, Jenny. I know I acted like a jerk these past few months. No wonder Grandma's so mad at me."

"She's worried about you."

"I don't deserve Chris," Heather said, sounding like her old self. "It's my own fault I lost him, Jenny. He's never coming back to me."

Jenny hugged her friend close, feeling sorry for her. She just hoped there was something better around the corner for Heather.

Chapter 10

"I think you should seize all the records in Gianni's office," Jenny argued with Adam. "Have some other doctor study them."

"And why would I do that?"

"You will get a list of all the people he scammed. Any of those could be a suspect."

"I talked to Dr. Smith about those scams," Adam told Jenny. "Gianni was just billing the government for work he didn't do. Most of the fake records deal with treatment that was not provided to his patients. I know it was illegal but it didn't hurt his patients."

"You can't be sure about that," Jenny persisted. "Some people got a wrong diagnosis. He might have written fake prescriptions that made their way to the patient. What if someone actually took the wrong medicine?"

"I can't go running after every wild scenario."

"This is plausible. Think about it a bit and you will agree with me."

"I'll look into it," Adam said in a resigned tone.

"What about Tiffany? Have you questioned her yet?"

"She's coming to town today for an interview."

"She's a woman scorned, Adam. She had a strong motive."

"Let me do my job, Jenny," Adam pleaded. "Please."

Jenny walked out of his office in a huff. She pulled out her cell phone as soon as she stepped out of the police station and called Tiffany Costa.

"Are you coming to Pelican Cove today? Can we meet?"

Jenny gave her directions for the Boardwalk Café and set up a time to meet.

The Magnolias came in for their mid-morning coffee. Betty Sue was looking better than she had in a long time.

"You look happy," Star observed. "What are you hiding, Betty Sue?"

Betty Sue put down her knitting and leaned toward Star.

"Heather talked to me last night. I think she's going to be okay."

"She's a good kid," Star agreed. "I told you she would come around."

Molly and Heather came in together, arm in arm. Molly looked like she was bursting to tell them something.

"I am meeting the parents," she beamed. "Chris is setting it up."

"You know old Pa Williams," Star said. "You have talked to him hundreds of times."

"Not as my prospective father-in-law," Molly said shyly. "I hope he likes me."

"Ma Williams is a good woman," Betty Sue told Molly. "She's going to love you."

"I've known her since I was a kid," Heather added. "I'll put in a good word for you, Molls."

The lunch crowd kept Jenny busy. Finally, she sat down to grab a bite with Petunia.

"Do you need any help with that cake?" the old woman asked.

"I got it, don't worry."

Jenny had started baking cakes for special occasions like birthdays and anniversaries. There was no super market in Pelican Cove where you could just pick up a cake on the fly. So Jenny's little cake business had taken off.

"What is it this time?" Petunia asked as she took a bite of her fried fish sandwich.

"Lemon cake with raspberry filling," Jenny told her, "like those cupcakes I made the other day. It's for a thirteen year old girl. I hope she likes the pink frosting."

Jenny's phone buzzed just then.

"I'm waiting for you. You can come any time."

Jenny hung up the phone and made a fresh sandwich for Tiffany. She took the plate and a pitcher of sweet tea out to the deck.

Tiffany Costa came in, looking like a young Marilyn Monroe. Petunia led her out to the deck.

"Fabulous view!" Tiffany said as she sat down.

Jenny pointed to the sandwich.

"I thought you might be hungry."

"You're a doll," Tiffany squealed. "I'm starving. That grumpy cop didn't even offer me a glass of water."

Jenny was familiar with the grumpy cop's behavior so she wasn't surprised.

Tiffany drained half the glass of tea in one gulp. She

attacked her sandwich as if she hadn't eaten in days. Jenny allowed her to settle down.

"The cops found out I was here at the restaurant," Tiffany said.

She narrowed her eyes and looked at Jenny.

"It's a small town. People can spot a stranger from a mile away."

"They asked me a ton of questions. I answered every one of them. I have nothing to hide."

"That's good for you, Tiffany," Jenny said encouragingly.

"What did you want to talk about?" Tiffany asked, wiping her mouth with a tissue.

"My friend Heather is a suspect in Gianni's murder," Jenny said. "Who am I kidding? The police really think she did it. I'm trying to help her out."

"Are you some kind of detective?"

"Not really," Jenny admitted. "I just talk to people and try to find out stuff."

"How can I help you?" Tiffany asked cagily. "You are not trying to incriminate me, are you?"

"I just want to find out the truth."

"I know most people point at the trophy wife," Tiffany bristled. "I'm not just a blonde bimbo, you know."

"Trust me, Tiffany," Jenny said. "You have nothing to worry about if you are innocent."

"Do you think I would be talking to you if I wasn't?" the girl asked.

Jenny decided not to answer that.

"Tell me about Gianni," Jenny urged. "Were you a patient of his? How did you two meet?"

"We met online," Tiffany said wistfully.

Her eyes had a faraway look as if she was remembering happier times.

"He was so handsome!"

"What were you doing at the time?"

"I worked as a dental hygienist in the city," Tiffany told her. "Gianni swept me off my feet. He took me to fancy restaurants, bought me pretty things. Then on Valentine's Day two years ago, he proposed."

"Were you surprised?"

"Not really," Tiffany said. "I have been chased by

117

many men. They always propose to me. It can get really boring."

"I am guessing it was different with Gianni?" Jenny quizzed.

Tiffany smiled.

"I wanted him to take the next step. We had a court wedding but he took me to Aruba for our honeymoon."

"What about your family?" Jenny asked.

"I come from a small town in the mountains," Tiffany explained. "I was raised by an old aunt. She's in long term care now. I don't have anyone else."

"Was he living in Delaware when you got married?"

"Oh yes. I had known that when we were dating."

"When did you learn about the affairs?"

"Two months after marriage," Tiffany said with a scowl. "Gianni was quite open about it. He said it was a ruse. He snared a local girl to get his foot into a new community."

"What about the shady activities? Did he tell you about them himself?"

"I helped him with some filing a couple of times," Tiffany explained. "I had noticed some odd things. But I was quiet about it. He started bragging about it one night when he was drunk."

"And you were fine with that?"

"I had never done anything illegal," Tiffany admitted. "But he gave me a diamond bracelet two days later. I said nothing."

"So he bought your silence."

Tiffany looked uncomfortable.

"I grew up dirt poor. I never had fancy things."

Jenny didn't torment her any further.

"Can I look at the files at your place?" she asked.

"Sure! You can come and get them any time."

"How long did Gianni plan to go out with Heather?"

"Pelican Cove turned out to be smaller than he had imagined. He said he had pretty much exhausted his options here. He had already hired a moving company. He was getting out of here by the end of February."

"What are your plans now?" Jenny asked her.

"I might get my old job back," Tiffany said. "Just to

stay busy."

Jenny told her she would visit soon to look at Gianni's files.

Tiffany didn't seem worried about her future. Gianni must have left her well off, Jenny mused as she walked to the seafood market. Chris greeted her with a brilliant smile.

"Hey, Jenny!"

Jenny called her aunt to ask her what she wanted for dinner.

"We have an extra guest," her aunt told her. "That's five for dinner."

Jenny picked up fresh peppers and mushrooms from the local farm. She doubled her usual order of fish and shrimp and remembered they were out of Old Bay seasoning.

"Molly's excited about meeting your parents," she told Chris.

Chris fingered his shiny new promise ring and blushed.

"She's a bit tense too. My mother scares her."

Jenny beamed as she thought of something.

"Why don't you all come to Seaview for dinner? Star will be there, and Jimmy and Adam. It will be a more casual setting."

"That's a great idea, Jenny," Chris said eagerly. "You sure you won't mind?"

"We haven't had company in a long time. Just tell me what your parents like to eat."

"They'll eat anything," he said. "Mom doesn't like spicy food though."

"I'll keep that in mind," Jenny promised. "Let me talk to my aunt and come up with a date. I'll call you."

Jenny was in for a surprise when she reached home. Star had set up an easel on the beach outside Seaview. There was another easel next to hers. Frank, the artist, was standing beside her aunt, brush in hand, talking about something.

"They are having a plain air session," Jimmy told her with a scowl. "That creep's been here since noon. And your aunt has been standing out there with him."

"You mean 'plein' air," Jenny laughed. "It's a French term for painting outdoors."

Jimmy sat in a chair on the patio, staring out at the beach. Jenny knew he wouldn't be easy to spot from the beach, but he had a clear view of Star and her companion.

"Is that the guest we are having for dinner?" Jenny asked.

"He invited himself," Jimmy grumbled. "Said he fancied a nice home cooked meal. He can cook it in his own kitchen, can't he?"

"I thought he lived in a bus."

"He travels in that bus. He's rented a house in town. The bus is parked in his yard."

"Star's just being nice," Jenny said with a smile.

She wondered what Jimmy was worried about. Although her aunt had never said it out loud, Jenny was sure she really liked Jimmy. She wasn't going to be impressed by some vagabond artist.

Adam came home and offered to help with dinner. Jenny gave him the job of chopping the vegetables. She sprinkled Old Bay on fish and drizzled it with olive oil. She set it aside, ready to go in the oven just before they sat down to eat.

"I met Tiffany today," Jenny told him. "Sounds like you were a bit harsh with her."

"I was just doing my job," Adam told her.

"Tiffany's offered to let me look at Gianni's old records."

"That's great," Adam said eagerly. "Dr. Smith is looking at the stuff we found here in Pelican Cove. But that's all I can do for now. The other stuff is off limits for me."

"Adam Hopkins," Jenny said with her hands on her hips. "Are you actually asking for my help?"

"You might be able to go where I can't," Adam said. "Who knows what those records will yield."

"Does Tiffany come into a lot of money?" Jenny asked.

"She's the spouse," Adam shrugged. "Unless we find a will or someone turns up with one, she is his next of kin."

"So she could have killed him for his money."

"We are trying to establish her alibi. We already know she was in town that night. Unless she can prove what time she left town, she had as much opportunity as Heather."

"She also had access to Gianni's clinic and all the drugs he kept there," Jenny reminded him.

Adam agreed with Jenny for a change. Tank came in

and sat down on the floor next to Jenny.

"Who's that dude out there with Star?" Adam asked. "And why is Jimmy hiding behind the rose bushes?"

Chapter 11

Adam Hopkins walked into the Boardwalk Café at noon.

"Hello Sheriff," Jenny smiled. "Taking the day off?"

"I'm here for lunch," Adam said. "Care to join me?"

Jenny ladled pea soup in two bowls and placed strawberry chicken sandwiches on a plate. She took the tray of food out to the deck. It was a sunny spring day and the fresh breeze coming off the ocean perked her up.

Adam slurped the soup and pronounced it delicious.

"I asked around," he told Jenny. "Old Asher Cohen had sponsored the toll both all those years ago. He paid the people who worked there."

Jenny's face fell.

"Asher's gone now."

"Asher may not be around but his company, Cohen Construction is," Adam reminded her. "I spoke to Luke."

Luke Stone was Jason's uncle. He ran Cohen

Construction, one of the biggest employers in town.

Jenny took a bite of her sandwich and nodded for Adam to go on.

"Asher was very meticulous about keeping records. Luke is sure they have everything from back when the booth was still running."

"When can I look at them?" Jenny asked eagerly.

"Luke's having someone pull them from their records section. You can go there later this afternoon. They are expecting you."

"Sounds great," Jenny said. "You think I'll find something?"

"Whatever you find will be something we don't know now," Adam told her. "Think of it as another piece of the puzzle."

"Yes Sir!" Jenny gave him a mock salute.

Her enthusiasm waned a bit when she saw the three foot high pile of paper set aside for her at Cohen Construction. She sat down and started looking for the right year.

Apparently, the toll booth had been operational for barely a year. It had never actually collected toll. Its only purpose had been to note down the cars entering and leaving the city. Jenny noted down the relevant information and struggled to her feet. Her legs were stiff after sitting in one spot for hours. She hoped the information she had found would provide some value.

Jenny walked back home, thinking about Lily. Lily had grown up in Pelican Cove. She had left town at nineteen and come back several years later with her husband and children. Her husband worked in the city and was traveling most of the time. Her daughter died from a freak virus. Lily's son was in college at that time. According to Betty Sue, Lily had shut herself in her house after her daughter's death. It didn't seem like she had any enemies. She hardly talked to anyone. Why had someone taken her life?

Jenny walked on for a while before she found herself in front of the library. She remembered something Betty Sue had said. Molly greeted her at the desk, looking radiant.

"Chris told me you are hosting us for dinner, Jenny," she beamed. "Thank you so much. To be honest, I was a bit intimidated at the thought of going to their home for dinner. But I'll feel right at home at Seaview."

Jenny spent some time chatting with Molly about the dinner party. She went in to the reference section and began looking at newspapers from 1991. There was no news item related to Lily's disappearance. Jenny found it odd. Why hadn't the Pelican Cove Chronicle printed anything about Lily? She moved to the classifieds section next. She spotted the ad for the sale of Seaview right away. Her eyes popped open at what she saw on the page. Had grief really addled Lily's brain?"

"Not a single car went out of town that night," she told Adam later that night.

They were taking a long walk on the beach after a rich dinner of Star's special six cheese lasagna. Tank ran in circles around them, begging Jenny to throw a stick he could fetch.

"Did anyone come into town?"

Jenny shook her head. "Not after 3 PM that day."

"Did you note those numbers?"

"I did more than that," Jenny told him. "Those same cars left town around 6:30 in the morning and got back by 4 PM. I am guessing these belonged to people who commuted to the mainland."

"Good guess," Adam complimented her. "What about the days before and after Lily disappeared?"

"I didn't see any car leaving town for a day after that."

"Are you saying Lily never got into a car?"

"I'm saying she didn't go out of town for sure," Jenny

said. "At least not that night. So this whole story about her running away with someone seems pretty thin now."

"She could have stayed with someone else in town for a couple of days," Adam mused.

"Betty Sue says Lily hardly spoke to anyone those days. I find it hard to believe she had a secret lover."

"So you believe Ann lied?"

"I don't know what to believe, Adam. But it's beginning to look probable. It's Ann's word against Lily's and Lily is not here to defend herself."

"Hmmm …"

Adam lapsed into silence. Tank nudged Jenny, trying to get her attention. She played with him for a while.

"And wait till you hear this," Jenny spoke up. "Lily wanted to sell Seaview. She listed it in the classifieds for twenty thousand dollars."

"What?" Adam exclaimed. "You sure you didn't miss a zero?"

Jenny shook her head.

"It was printed in words too, Adam. I know things were cheaper back then, but surely not that cheap?"

"Why would Lily do that?"

"Betty Sue said she just wanted to get away from here."

"Do you remember Ann and her son owned half the house? I'm sure they didn't go along with that."

"Lily was acting erratic, that's for sure."

Jenny couldn't wait to tell the Magnolias all she had found out. She waited impatiently for Betty Sue's arrival the next morning. Betty Sue walked in, busy knitting something pink.

"Sit down, Betty Sue. I want to ask you something."

"How about some coffee first, eh?" Betty Sue grumbled. "What's got you so twisted?"

Jenny poured out her story.

"Twenty thousand dollars!" Betty Sue exclaimed. "There was a recession around that time but Seaview was worth several times more than that."

"How come someone didn't snap up the property?" Jenny asked her.

A knowing look flashed across Betty Sue's face.

"It was the curse. People around here believed Seaview

was jinxed."

"Did Ann want to sell too?"

"Ann came here and liked what she saw. She wanted to live here with Ricky."

"But they went back!"

"I never understood why," Betty Sue nodded. "You can ask Ann about it. She was as eager to stay on here as Lily was to leave."

"Did they get along?" Jenny asked.

"Lily adored Ann when we were teenagers," Betty Sue said. "She was young, sophisticated and married, everything we aspired to as girls. Ann could do no wrong in Lily's eyes."

"Didn't Lily live with Ann for a while?"

"Those two were pretty close once upon a time," Betty Sue agreed.

"But not in 1991?"

"Lily was really hard to be around that time," Betty Sue said reluctantly. "Her mood swings had become really hard to take. She would throw tantrums at the slightest provocation. She didn't talk to a single person for days together. She sat on the balcony at Seaview, staring at the sea, sobbing her heart out for her girl."

"Ann stayed here through all that?"

"She did," Betty Sue said grimly. "She held the family together."

Jenny wondered if Ann Davis had really loved Lily.

Molly and Heather came in, arm in arm.

"Are you all set for this special dinner?" Heather asked with a smile. "Let me know if you need any help. I can give you the skinny on what Chris's mother likes."

"Thanks Heather," Jenny said. "I'm almost ready, I think. Chris is coming around with the fish around four."

"That takes care of the food," Heather said. "What are you wearing, Molly?"

"That new green dress?" Molly said uncertainly.

"Mrs. Williams likes blue. Don't you have a blue dress you can wear?" Heather was trying really hard to be likable. "What about your hair?"

"It's just a dinner, Heather," Jenny rolled her eyes. "Stop scaring Molly."

"I know, but you know what they say about first

impressions."

"You're making me nervous," Molly said, beginning to look green. "I tend to puke when I get nervous."

"We can't have that," Heather frowned. "Just be your usual self, Molls. You got this."

Star had set up her easel on the patio when Jenny got home. She was muttering to herself.

"What are you doing, Star?" Jenny laughed.

"I'm trying my hand at water colors," she said. "Not as easy as it looks."

"I thought you hated them."

"I never really gave them a shot. Frank says watercolor is actually the most difficult medium."

"Frank says, huh?"

"A true artist does not shy away from different techniques. Frank says I should think of adding water colors to my portfolio."

"When did you go shopping for all these new colors?"

"Frank lent them to me. He's quite generous, that one."

"Carry on then," Jenny told her aunt. "I have my work

cut out for me."

"Are we having company?" Star asked. "I was thinking of asking Frank over for dinner."

"Have you forgotten Molly's dinner party?" Jenny asked her, rubbing a charm around her neck.

She had been missing Nick all day.

"Oh yeah," Star said. "That's tonight? Why didn't you say so earlier?" Star began putting away her stuff. "I'll help you in the kitchen."

Molly's party started off well. Heather had kept her word and helped Molly get ready. Molly was wearing more makeup than usual and she kept touching her face every few minutes.

"Relax," Jenny whispered in her ear.

Pa Williams, Chris's father, was an easy going man. He put an arm around Molly and welcomed her to the family. His wife didn't seem that forthcoming. Her face had a pinched expression.

"She's not a Pioneer," she said to Star. "You know how we feel about that."

A peculiar hierarchy existed on the island of Pelican Cove. A bunch of families who had been the original settlers called themselves the Pioneers. Only five or six families had this honor. The Morse family, Betty Sue and Heather's ancestors were one of them, being the original owners of the island. So were the Stone and Williams families. They had been on the island since the nineteenth century.

Molly's family came from a group called the refugees. Her family had sought shelter in Pelican Cove after the great storm of 1962, a deadly storm which had wrought massive destruction up and down the coast.

Time didn't move very fast in Pelican Cove. Family background mattered a lot.

"Your son loves this girl," Star hissed. "Can't you be happy about that?"

Star herself was a chicken necker, a term the islanders used for someone who wasn't born there. She had come to Pelican Cove in the 1970s and never gone back.

"You wouldn't understand," Mrs. Williams told Star. "And what is this love you speak of? My son was in love with Heather Morse since third grade. I don't know how this girl managed to snare him."

Molly overheard them and turned red. Her eyes filled up and threatened to spill over. Jenny took her by the arm and led her inside.

"She doesn't like me," Molly stuttered.

A wild look had come into her eyes.

"I can't marry Chris without their blessing. What am I going to do?"

"She's in shock," Jenny soothed. "Your engagement is kind of sudden."

"We are not even engaged," Molly cried. "And now his mother doesn't approve of me."

"Chris loves you," Jenny said firmly. "He's going to stand by you no matter what, Molls."

"Do you really believe that, Jenny?"

Jenny crossed her fingers behind her back and nodded at her friend.

Chapter 12

"Jenny, it's for you," Petunia called out.

Jenny put down the piping bag she was holding and answered the phone.

"This is Dr. Smith. You gave me this number."

"How are you, Doc?" Jenny greeted him. "Any update?"

"Can you come down to my clinic?"

"Give me an hour," Jenny said and hung up.

She immediately dialed Jason's number.

"I don't know what he's come up with. Do you want to go with me?"

Jason pulled up outside the Boardwalk Café half an hour later. Jason seemed to have lost weight since the last time Jenny saw him. There were dark circles under his eyes.

"Are you ill?" she asked with concern. "What's wrong?"

"Haven't been sleeping well," Jason said with a shrug.

"When was the last time you had a proper meal?" Jenny asked suspiciously. "That's it. You're coming to Seaview for dinner tonight."

"Whatever you say, Jenny," he mumbled.

They reached Dr. Smith's clinic ten minutes later. He was waiting for them.

"I went through most of Costa's records," he said. "I found more of what we saw before."

Jenny sensed there was more coming.

"One of the names seemed familiar," Dr. Smith sighed. "Eugenie Hampton. She died recently."

"How did she die?"

"I checked her death certificate," Dr. Smith said grimly. "She died of heart failure."

"I remember reading her obit," Jason said.

"Was she your patient, Dr. Smith?" Jenny asked.

"Was is the operative word," the doctor said bitterly. "I treated Eugenie Hampton for forty years. She started seeing Costa last winter."

"Any reason why?"

"He charmed her, I guess," Dr. Smith said. "Some of

my patients started seeing him recently. I couldn't stop them."

"I'm guessing most of these were women of a certain age?" Jenny asked. "Did Eugenie have any chronic conditions?"

"I'm not supposed to discuss my patients with anyone," Dr. Smith reminded them. "But I can tell you this. I saw the treatment Costa was supposedly giving her. It was all wrong for her."

"So he actually gave someone wrong medicine?" Jenny asked, aghast. "But you said he was just billing the government for this extra stuff."

"Looks like he was doing more than that," Dr. Smith said. "Or there was some error in the paperwork. She saw something she was not meant to see and filled those prescriptions. Taking those drugs might have led to her demise."

"Can you prove that?"

"It will be hard to prove without an autopsy."

"Did she have any family?" Jason asked.

"Her husband lives in town," Dr. Smith said. "He's still my patient. I can give you his address."

"Let's go talk to him," Jenny said to Jason.

Peter Hampton was home when they went to see him. He was sitting out on his porch in a rocker, staring at a bird feeder that hung from an old oak.

Jason introduced himself.

"I know who you are," he grunted. "What do you want?"

"We wanted to talk to you about your wife."

"She's dead," he said. "Are you going to let me mourn her in peace?"

"We just want a few minutes of your time," Jenny pleaded.

The man paid no attention and continued staring in the distance.

"Maybe we'll come back some other time," Jason said.

He took Jenny's arm and led her back to the car.

"You are giving up?" she protested as he started the car.

"He won't talk to us right now," Jason said.

"I want to tell Adam about this guy. Why don't you drop me off there?"

Jason pulled up outside the police station a few

minutes later.

"See you at seven sharp," Jenny said primly. "Bring your appetite."

Adam was immersed in some paperwork when Jenny breezed into his office.

"You have a new suspect," she declared.

Adam looked at her irritably.

"What are you blathering about, Jenny?"

"I'm talking about Gianni's murder. I just found a new suspect for you."

"Pray tell," Adam drawled.

"A woman called Eugenie Hampton died from the wrong medicine. I just saw her husband. He refused to talk to me."

"Genie's dead?" Adam sat up, surprised. "She used to be friends with my mom."

"Her husband looks devastated. Dr. Smith says she probably died from a wrong prescription. That gives her husband a motive."

"All this makes a fine story, Jenny," Adam said patiently. "But I need proof."

"Isn't it your job to get that?" Jenny shot back.

"I don't know, Jenny. Sounds farfetched to me."

Jenny stormed out of Adam's office and started walking home. She spotted Captain Charlie coming out of The Steakhouse. He was holding a small bag of food.

"Just delivered the catch," he told her. "The chef made me dinner."

"Do you know a man called Peter Hampton?"

"Aye."

"Can you find out if he came to The Steakhouse recently?"

"What are you up to, little lady?" Captain Charlie asked.

He went inside the restaurant again. Jenny tapped her foot impatiently while she waited for him to come out.

"He was here," Captain Charlie grunted when he came out. "One of the busboys told me."

"Are they sure? Do they know who he is?"

"Pete Hampton's lived here all his life," Captain Charlie quipped. "That's seventy some years you have not been here, missy. Most people around here know him well."

"What was he doing here?"

A lad walked out just then, pulling off his apron. Captain Charlie summoned him over.

"Tell her what you saw."

"Old Pete Hampton came here for dinner for Valentine's Day. It was kinda sad. We all know his wife passed."

"Was it Valentine's Day or the day after?" Jenny asked eagerly.

The lad shrugged.

"Could have been either. It was some time that weekend." He stared at Jenny for a few seconds. "I know you. You were in here with that big group. Pete was here the same day as you."

"Did he talk to anyone?"

"He was talking to that dude with the diamond earring."

The lad looked bored. He said a hasty goodbye and walked away from them rapidly.

"Does that help?" Captain Charlie asked.

"More than you know," Jenny told him, grinning from ear to ear.

She couldn't wait to talk to Adam. Jenny hurried through her dinner prep. Star had invited her new artist friend so there were six of them for dinner. Jenny made a big pot of gumbo to go around. She hoped Frank liked spicy food.

"Pete Hampton was at The Steakhouse with us," she told Adam as soon as he came home. "He was right there."

"Gianni didn't die in the restaurant, Jenny."

"But he could have been poisoned there."

"He wasn't. Trust me on that. I can't tell you any more than that now."

Jenny tried to make Jason talk during dinner. He ate a few spoonfuls of gumbo and pushed his plate away.

Jenny tried to hide her concern.

"Will you pick me up at nine tomorrow morning?" she asked him.

"Sure," he agreed.

Frank was asking Star to dinner.

"You have made me feel so welcome. I am taking you to dinner and I won't take no for an answer."

Star tried to hide a blush.

"Your aunt is so talented," he gushed, looking at Jenny. "She just started using water colors two days ago and her work is already better than mine."

"Oh Frank, stop it!" Star said, turning red.

Jimmy Parsons stared at them with a scowl on his face. It was clear he wasn't dealing well with the interloper.

Jason arrived at the café at nine the next morning. Jenny handed him a box with a giant chocolate cupcake. Jason's face broke into a smile.

"So you can still smile," Jenny teased. "Why didn't you say you wanted cake?"

"Where to?" Jason wanted to know.

Jenny told him what she had discovered the previous day.

"We are going to see Peter Hampton again. And this time I am not going to budge until he starts talking."

Peter Hampton was sitting in the same spot on his

porch, staring at the bird feeder again. His brow furrowed when he spotted them.

"Didn't I tell you to clear off?" he roared.

"We need to talk, Mr. Hampton," Jenny said with her hands on her hips. "What were you doing at The Steakhouse?"

"It's a free country," the old man sneered. "I was getting a meal."

"You were doing more than that."

Peter Hampton folded his hands and looked away.

"Look, we are sorry about your wife," Jenny began.

"We were married for fifty six years," the man said. A single tear rolled down his eye. "I was supposed to take care of her."

"You couldn't have known," Jenny said gently.

"He had all those fancy certificates," Peter said. "My Genie said Dr. Smith was getting old. This Gianni fellow had access to all the latest technology. He promised he would make her sciatica go away. She believed him."

"He was giving fake prescriptions," Jenny stated. "When did you find out?"

"Not until it was too late," Peter Hampton said bitterly. "That Costa fellow said it was my Genie's fault. She couldn't read, he said. She was never supposed to take those pills."

"You went to The Steakhouse to cause a scene, didn't you?"

Peter Hampton straightened in his chair. His eyes hardened.

"I was prepared to do more than that. I was carrying a knife under my jacket. I was going to kill that bastard in the restroom."

"What happened?" Jason asked, fascinated.

He was finally beginning to act like his old self.

"I chickened out," the man said. "I couldn't do it. I couldn't kill a man in cold blood."

"Even though he was responsible for your wife's death?" Jenny pressed.

"I failed my Genie," Peter said. Tears were flowing down his face freely now. "How am I going to face her?"

"You did the right thing," Jason said, patting the man on his back.

"Did you argue with Gianni that day?" Jenny asked.

"I let him have it," Peter nodded. "He laughed at me. Said small town folks were gullible."

"Did you follow him home?" Jenny pressed.

"No Ma'am," Peter shook his head. "I went to the Rusty Anchor to drown myself in a bottle."

"Did anyone see you there?"

"Eddie Cotton did, I guess," Peter said with a frown. "And a bunch of other people in the bar. Why?"

"Never mind," Jenny said. "Mr. Hampton, can I bring you a casserole some time?"

"You are the girl from the café, aren't you? My Genie loved your waffles."

Jenny was quiet on the way back.

"You miss her, don't you?" she asked, placing her hand on Jason's.

"What happened, Jenny?" Jason asked, his eyes full of pain. "Where did I go wrong?"

"You could never go wrong, my friend," Jenny said fiercely.

"I tried calling her a few times," Jason admitted. "She

won't answer my calls."

"You know how busy Kandy is," Jenny said. "Maybe she's working on some high profile case and doesn't want to be disturbed."

Jason shook his head.

"Her email clearly said we were done."

"Coward!" Jenny spit out.

She had never been impressed with Kandy's bossy personality.

"Can't you forget her, Jason?" she asked. "There's plenty of fish in the sea."

"I didn't go looking for anyone," Jason said bitterly. "She pursued me. And now she's backing out."

"It might be for the best," Jenny said with a shrug. "If she's so flighty, it's better you found out now."

"I wasn't completely honest with her," Jason said after a while. "I think she sensed that."

"What do you mean?" Jenny asked, bewildered.

"Kandy and I, we were hanging out, Jenny," Jason stuttered. "But I was, I am, in love with someone else."

Chapter 13

Jimmy Parsons walked into the Boardwalk Café. He wasn't a café regular.

"This is a surprise," Jenny said, welcoming him. "What can I get you, Jimmy?"

"I guess I'll have a cup of coffee, with cream and sugar."

"How about some breakfast? I am making waffles."

"Why not?" Jimmy shrugged.

He seemed agitated.

"Okay, out with it," Jenny said, placing a plate of waffles drizzled with her special berry sauce before Jimmy. "What's on your mind?"

"It's your aunt," Jimmy began. "Do you think she's sweet on this new artist fellow?"

Jenny burst out laughing.

"What makes you think that?"

"He's taking her to dinner tonight, to the Steakhouse, no less."

"I think she's just being polite."

"She can't stop talking about him," Jimmy grumbled. "It's Frank this or Frank that."

"She never gets to meet any fellow artists," Jenny offered. "It's just shop talk."

"I hope that's all it is."

Jimmy gazed moodily at his waffles and took a bite. Jenny took pity on him.

"She likes you, Jimmy. I know that much for sure."

Jenny decided to talk to her aunt later. The Magnolias came in and settled at their favorite table on the deck.

"You are coming to the town meeting, aren't you?" Heather asked Jenny. "We need a good turnout."

"Are you working with Barb now?" Jenny asked.

"She needs an assistant and I am at a loose end," Heather explained. "Plus, I feel strongly about this drugs issue."

"Calling it a 'drugs issue' gives the wrong impression," Jenny said.

"Come to the town hall meeting to voice your opinion," Heather quipped. "It's an open forum. We will let everyone speak their mind."

Jenny was glad to see Heather taking an interest in something other than men.

"How was the party at your place?" Betty Sue wanted to know.

"Jenny did a great job," Molly praised. "Chris said his father likes me."

No one wanted to talk about his mother.

"I heard about your hot date," Jenny told Star. "What do you see in that guy?"

"How do you know about it?" Star asked. She looked embarrassed. "He was quite persuasive. I couldn't say no."

"Jimmy was here this morning."

"What's he doing, talking about my business?" Star asked crossly. "I need to talk to that Jimmy."

"I think he feels left out," Jenny said. "It's cute."

"Frank's just like a tourist. He'll be gone in a few months."

"As long as you don't take off with him ..."

Jenny was tossing salad for lunch when the phone

rang. It was Tiffany, Gianni Costa's wife.

"You said you wanted to look at Gianni's records?" she asked Jenny. "I've put everything in a few boxes and set it aside for you. You can come and get them anytime."

Jenny told her she would come by later that day. She called Jason and asked him if he was up for a road trip.

"Who's this?" Tiffany asked as she gave Jason a once over.

"Jason lives in Pelican Cove. I rode with him today."

Jason was being his old charming self. He chatted up Tiffany.

"I was planning to leave my husband," she told Jason. "He was seeing other women on the side."

"That must have been hard on you," Jason commiserated.

"I was just a poor working girl when I met Gianni. I had nowhere to go."

"You never said you wanted to leave Gianni?" Jenny asked her.

"I put on a brave front," Tiffany shrugged. "No wife can tolerate a cheating husband. I gave him an ultimatum."

"You did?" Jenny humored her.

"He had to stop seeing this Heather girl or I was walking out."

"What did Gianni say?"

"He laughed at me. Said I was free to walk out any time I wanted."

"Did you sign any prenuptial agreement?" Jason asked.

"Jason's a lawyer," Jenny added.

"I did sign something," Tiffany said with a shrug. "But I didn't understand much of it. Gianni said I would be taken care of."

"I can take a look at it if you want me to," Jason offered.

Tiffany went in and came out with a folder.

"It's all in there."

Jason didn't need a lot of time to skim through the papers. He shook his head and gave them back to Tiffany.

"According to this, you get nothing if you leave your husband."

"Even if he cheated on me?"

"If you walk out, you don't get a penny, no matter what the reason is."

"That's not fair," Jenny said.

"Gianni said this was just a formality," Tiffany said, incensed. "I was so much in love, I didn't give it a second thought."

"What did you do later that night at the Steakhouse?" Jenny asked her.

"I was starving, but I didn't want to stay in that place for one moment more than necessary. I drove back home to Delaware."

"Alone?"

"Of course! Gianni was too busy canoodling with that tart."

"You didn't talk to Gianni at all that night?"

Tiffany shook her head.

"I'm sure he saw me there."

Jenny wanted to use the restroom. Tiffany pointed down the hallway. Jenny peeped into a powder room and walked on, taking note of the other rooms. She saw a door leading down a small path through a garden. It led to a separate building that looked like a guesthouse. Jenny went inside the bathroom and flushed the toilet. She opened a faucet for a few minutes and came out, wiping her hands.

"Do you like to swim?" she asked Tiffany. "I thought I saw a pool house."

"That's not a pool house," Tiffany pouted. "That's Gianni's clinic. It's actually a guest house."

"So he could walk to and fro between his house and workplace whenever he wanted."

"So could I," Tiffany said with a nod. "It was … convenient."

"Okay," Jenny said, standing up. "We'll get these boxes out of your way."

They stopped at a small fish and chips shop on the way back. Jenny bit into hot beer battered fish and stared moodily at the water.

"You have to convince the police that Tiffany is a suspect. That might take the spotlight away from Heather."

"Give me one reason why she's a suspect," Jason said, dipping a French fry in ketchup.

"I'll give you three," Jenny said, holding up three fingers. "Never underestimate a woman scorned. Gianni cheated on her. I don't care what she says, she must have been raving mad."

"Go on," Jason said, taking a swig of his soda.

"As you said, she didn't stand to gain anything if she left Gianni. But she inherits his entire ill gotten gains as a widow."

"And you think that was the motive? Money?"

"Money or revenge," Jenny said with a shrug. "Call it what you will."

"How did she do it?" Jason asked.

"I don't know about that," Jenny said. "But she had access to Gianni's clinic. She could have ground up any combination of pills. She had plenty of opportunity."

"And how did she feed him this deadly cocktail?" Jason asked.

"I don't have all the answers," Jenny admitted. "Why not leave something for the police?"

"So she had a strong motive and she had the means," Jason summed up. "What about opportunity?"

"She was right there at the Steakhouse," Jenny cried.

"She could have easily walked to Gianni's place from there."

"That does put her on the scene," Jason agreed. "Has she given any alibi to the police?"

"I don't think they ever asked her for one."

"Why is your boyfriend convinced Heather is guilty?" Jason asked. "He's known her since she was a little girl. How could he believe her capable of something so heinous?"

"You know what Adam will say," Jenny said with exasperation. "He's just doing his job."

"I'm going to talk to him about Tiffany. She can't be ruled out as a suspect."

"You're Heather's lawyer," Jenny said with a nod. "You can talk to Adam in an official capacity. He will have to listen to you."

Groups of people were walking toward the town hall when they entered Pelican Cove.

"I forgot all about the meeting tonight," Jenny said. "You are coming, right?"

She held up her hand guessing Jason was about to say no.

"It will be fun, if nothing else."

Betty Sue sat on the stage near the front of the hall. John Newbury, her estranged husband, sat next to her. Ada Newbury sat in a corner seat, glaring at the crowd. Barb Norton stood behind the podium, calling the meeting to order. Heather stood at the back with a clipboard in her hand.

The Magnolias occupied the second row. They had saved room for Jenny and Jason.

"Thank you for coming," Barb began. "We need to raise a united voice against drugs in Pelican Cove. Thank you for signing the petition. I am sure it's going to help quash this whole thing."

"Why are we here then?" someone shouted from the crowd.

"I want to make sure every opinion is heard," Barb said pompously. "Although I am acting in the interest of the town, I'm no autocrat. And we want to tell the Newburys what we are thinking and what our concerns are."

An old woman sitting in the first row struggled to her feet, leaning heavily on a walking stick.

"I hear this marivana is going to help my knees. Is that true?"

"That's right," John Newbury spoke. "Marijuana helps in pain relief. We are going to grow high grade cannabis that will be processed into pills you can take for your arthritis."

"Where are you going to sell this?" another woman asked.

"We have leased a shop on Main Street," John replied.

"Main Street is where our kids hang out," a man said. "Minor kids. This dispensary as you call it is a bad influence on them."

Another man piped up from the crowd.

"What about ground water? I hear growing marijuana can contaminate ground water resources."

People started talking among themselves. Barb Norton tried to get their attention.

"One at a time, please."

"We don't want Pelican Cove to become a drug hangout," one man roared.

"You want to teach our kids it's okay to take drugs?" another woman demanded. "What kind of example are you setting for them?"

"You are just doing this to fill your pockets," an old

woman quavered.

John Newbury stood up to answer them. Someone threw a rotten tomato at him. An egg or two followed. Barb Norton tried in vain to get everyone to behave. Someone pelted her with popcorn.

The meeting pretty much derailed after that.

"What the heck was that?" Jenny asked Star on the way home. "I didn't know people here could be so violent."

"That's just your regular town hall meeting," Star laughed.

"I don't feel like cooking tonight. Let's just order in some pizza from Mama Rosa's."

"Sounds like a plan," Star said. "Will you get my favorite?"

"Chicken, jalapeno and pineapple, I know," Jenny assured her aunt. "Jimmy's started liking it too."

Star scrunched up her face at the mention of Jimmy.

"I've been thinking," she said. "I haven't spent much time with Jimmy lately."

"He's just feeling left out," Jenny said.

"Jimmy's not the kind to throw money around," Star

said.

Jenny knew what she was implying. Jimmy Parsons had a bunch of cottages he rented to tourists. He didn't have any other job. Jimmy wasn't rolling in money. It hadn't mattered to Star.

"Why don't you do something simple?" Jenny suggested. "The weather's warming up. Go for a picnic on the beach. I can make up a basket for you."

"That sounds romantic," Star sighed. "You think that will make him smile?"

"You just need to convince him he's special. He's gonna love it."

"Okay then," Star said happily. "I know the perfect place for a picnic."

"Do you need any talking points?" Jenny asked saucily.

"I don't, kid," Star said, rolling her eyes. "And I won't mention Frank at the picnic."

Chapter 14

The Magnolias were all quiet for a change. Betty Sue sipped her coffee and went on knitting furiously. Molly's head was buried in a book. Heather's eyes were rimmed with red. Petunia sat staring at them, crumpling a tissue in her hands. Star walked up the café steps, holding a few canvases.

"I'm taking these to the gallery," she told Jenny. "They are from my plein air session with Frank."

Jenny tipped her head at the women and gave her aunt a pleading look.

"What's the matter, Betty Sue?" Star boomed.

"I just got back from the police station," Heather said, blowing her nose in a tissue. "They wanted to question me again."

"What?" Jenny exclaimed. "I thought they had found other suspects."

"Apparently not," Heather said. "I'm still at the top of their list."

"I need to talk to Adam," Jenny said purposefully. "I'm going over right now."

"I'm coming with you," Betty Sue declared, discarding her knitting on the table. "I need to give that Hopkins boy a piece of my mind."

"That's not necessary, Betty Sue," Jenny said, dismayed. "Let me take care of this."

"You think I'm gonna cramp your style, girl?" Betty Sue thundered.

"Of course not," Jenny hastened to calm her down. "But I have a bone to pick with Adam. It might get ugly."

"Call me if you need me," Betty Sue relented.

"Of course," Jenny assured her.

She skipped down the café steps to the boardwalk and started walking toward the police station at a brisk pace.

Nora, the desk clerk, looked up when Jenny entered the station.

"I'm the one in a bad mood today," Jenny cautioned, holding up a hand.

Nora shrugged and shook her head.

"You know where to go."

Adam was eating a late breakfast at his desk.

"Hey Jenny," he greeted her. "This quiche is delicious. Never thought of myself as a quiche man."

"When will you stop harassing Heather?" Jenny cut to the chase.

She pulled up a chair and sat down with a thud. She crossed her arms and glared at Adam.

Adam looked at her coolly.

"I'm not harassing her as you say. I'm just questioning her which is routine in an investigation."

"Didn't Jason talk to you?" Jenny pressed. "I thought we provided you with other suspects."

"I did talk to Jason. But Heather is still a suspect too."

"But why?"

"I have my reasons, Jenny. I don't need to disclose them to you."

"What about Mr. Hampton's alibi? Did you check it out?"

"I talked to Eddie Cotton," Adam sighed. "The old man was at the pub until Eddie closed it for the night. He walked him home after that. Pete Hampton wasn't feeling too good. He was sick multiple times. Eddie stayed with him. They were up almost all night. Eddie didn't go home until morning."

"That clears the old man, I guess," Jenny said reluctantly.

"I talked to him, Jenny. I know what he was planning to do that night. But it wasn't his hand that killed the doctor. I am sure of that."

"What about Tiffany? She had means, motive and opportunity."

"She also has an alibi, Jenny."

"She had access to drugs and she also had access to Gianni's house here. She could have gone there from the restaurant."

"She left The Steakhouse while we were still there. She must have reached her home in Delaware before we left the restaurant."

"How do you know that?"

"She stopped for coffee on the way. She's on camera. That's the kind of proof we cannot ignore."

"How do you know she didn't come back into Pelican Cove?"

"I don't think she did, Jenny."

"How did Gianni die?" Jenny asked Adam. "You said he was drugged but when did that happen. And how?"

"There's a reason why we haven't released that information."

"Is it because you don't have a clue yourself?"

Adam began to look frustrated.

"You're being a nuisance, Jenny. Why don't you get back to the café and let me get on with my work?"

"Heather's been crying her eyes out."

"She has nothing to worry if she's innocent."

"You've known her all your life, Adam. Do you really think she's capable of killing someone?"

"The evidence against her is pretty strong. As an officer of the law, I cannot overlook it."

"Her relationship with Gianni wasn't a secret. Tiffany admitted she knew about it too. And Heather really liked Gianni. What possible motive could she have to kill him?"

"If I had to guess, I would say revenge."

"You need to do more than guess, Adam."

"We found Heather's fingerprints on the scene, on the very glass that contained the drugs, as a matter of fact."

"Heather's been in and out of that house for the past few weeks. She must have handled many things there."

Adam rubbed his forehead with his fingers.

"She had a prescription for antidepressants."

"Haven't you listened to anything I told you?" Jenny cried. "Gianni wrote up wrong prescriptions. It was a scam he was running."

"This is a real prescription written by Dr. Smith," Adam said gravely. "Heather admitted she filled that prescription. She even has a half empty bottle with her."

"So she took the pills herself!"

"We don't know that," Adam shrugged. "Those pills match one of the drugs found in Gianni's system. Heather could have ground up those pills and added them to Gianni's drink."

Jenny sat back in shock. Adam continued his onslaught.

"Heather had free access to Gianni's clinic here. Using the argument you use against Tiffany, Heather had access to plenty of drugs."

"You honestly believe she's guilty, don't you?"

"My feelings don't matter here, Jenny. The law only looks at the evidence. Things don't look too good for Heather right now."

"My money's still on Tiffany," Jenny insisted, scrambling to her feet. "She lied multiple times. First she told me Gianni had affairs all the time and she didn't care about them. Then she said she was going to leave Gianni because he cheated on her. Based on her prenup, she wasn't going to get a penny if she walked out on him. That's why she killed him. Now she inherits his fortune. Thanks to cops like you, she's roaming free."

"Tiffany had a prenuptial agreement?" Adam asked. "I didn't know about that."

"I'm sure there is plenty more you don't know, Sheriff," Jenny said as she stomped out.

Jenny's anger subsided as soon as she stepped out of the police station. It was replaced by worry for her friend. She crossed the road and walked into Jason Stone's office.

Jason was talking to someone on the phone.

"Kandy and I were invited to a dinner party," he said stoically. "I was calling to tell them I won't be making it."

"I can go with you," Jenny offered.

"Not this time," Jason sighed. "It was for introducing Kandy to my college buddies."

"Oh."

"All well, Jenny? What brings you here at this time of the day?"

"I think Heather's in trouble," Jenny blurted out. "I just spoke to Adam."

"Did he tell you about finding her fingerprints on the scene?" Jason asked.

Jenny nodded.

"Things are not looking good, Jason. What will happen if this case goes to court?"

"I'm not a criminal lawyer, Jenny. But I can recommend one of the best persons for this job."

"Can you negotiate a lighter sentence if Heather admits she did it?"

Jason pursed his mouth.

"We should not be talking about this."

"I'm thinking of the worst case scenario here, Jason."

"I can see that. Heather's calling the shots here Jenny. She's my client, not you."

"Let me know if I can help," Jenny offered. "I'm going to keep working on this."

Jenny walked back to the café, feeling helpless. Adam had been so confident she was beginning to doubt Heather's innocence.

She spent the day feeling cranky, even snapping at a couple of tourists who wanted more salt in their soup. She had a splitting headache by the time she got home.

A couple of duffel bags lay on the front porch. Adam sat in a chair, looking at his watch and tapping his foot. Tank leapt at Jenny when he saw her, placing his paws on her shoulders.

Jenny hugged and kissed him.

"I've had a bad day, Tank," she whispered in his ear.

She finally noticed the bags.

"Do we have guests?" she questioned. "Wait a minute, has Nick turned up with some of his friends?"

Those are my bags, Jenny," Adam said calmly. "I'm going home."

"What? No!" Jenny wailed.

She stared at Adam with a wild look in her eyes.

"When did you decide that?"

"We talked about this," Adam said softly. "The contractors moved out of my house a couple of weeks ago."

"But we never talked about a date. Why today?"

"Why not?"

"You can't spring this on me, Adam. Not after the day I've had."

"I'm sorry, Jenny. The twins are coming home this weekend. I want to air the place out before that. Stock the refrigerator."

"The twins are welcome here," Jenny said in a shocked voice. "I have always loved having them here."

Adam took Jenny by the shoulders and forced her to sit down.

"This is hard for me too, Jenny. You think I want to go?"

"Then don't."

"It's not right," Adam said with a shake of his head. "I've imposed on your hospitality for too long. People are beginning to talk, and I don't like it."

"I don't care what people say."

"But I do. I feel guilty about it."

"Is this because we fought before? Is this your way of punishing me?"

"Of course not, Jenny. How can you say that?"

"Then don't go," Jenny said mulishly. "Not today."

"You are going to feel the same any time I go, Jenny. It's got to be done some time."

"I was going to arrange a farewell party for you."

"There's no need for that. I'm not going anywhere. I will probably be here for dinner very often."

Tank sensed the tension in the air. He butted Jenny in the knee, and sat down at her feet.

"Tank doesn't want to go," Jenny declared.

"He can stay here," Adam said. "I can't."

"What can I say to make you change your mind?" Jenny's eyes filled up. She was trying hard to control herself.

"Please don't be like this, Jenny. There are some things

I can't do while I am still living here."

"What things?" Jenny asked, bewildered.

"You'll find out soon," Adam promised. "It's a surprise. Now dry your tears and see me off with a smile."

"You're sure you're not mad at me?" Jenny asked.

"Of course not," Adam promised. "I'll see you soon."

Adam picked up his bags and limped to his car. Tank refused to get up.

"He needs you, Tank," Jenny whispered. "Go take care of him."

Tank gave a tiny whine and followed Adam.

Jenny waved madly until Adam was out of sight. Then she felt silly. Adam was only going a couple of miles further. But she had grown used to living in the same house with him.

Star came out of the house and hugged her.

"We need a girls' night," she declared. "I'm calling the reinforcements."

Molly arrived half an hour later with Petunia in tow. Heather and Betty Sue were next.

Heather waved a bunch of DVDs in the air.

"I got all your favorites, Jenny. Start popping the corn."

"I'm making my twice baked macaroni and cheese," Star announced. "Molly's taking care of dessert."

"Banana splits with hot fudge and my special brownies," Molly promised.

"We are going to drive that Hopkins boy out of your mind, girl," Betty Sue cackled.

Jenny let her friends pamper her, trying not to think about what kind of surprise Adam had in store for her.

Chapter 15

The Magnolias were busy. Heather and Molly were assembling pimento cheese sandwiches. Star spooned crab salad on crackers and garnished them with a sprig of dill. Jenny was frosting tray after tray of cupcakes.

"I have to say, the Newburys don't do anything half-heartedly," Petunia said, bobbing her head. Her double chins wobbled as she looked around, making sure everything looked good.

"They are generous, aren't they?" Jenny said, sweeping a hand over the food. "They are paying for all this food for the whole town."

"They see it as an investment," Betty Sue snorted. "They stand to earn millions from that drug business."

There was another meeting in the town hall that evening. The Newburys had taken note of all the objections that had been raised by the people. They were going to address all those concerns.

Ada Newbury had hired the Boardwalk Café to provide refreshments for the meeting. Jenny and her friends had been busy making sure the food matched Ada's specific instructions.

The town hall was packed. People were gorging on the

food. Some openly admitted coming there just for the food. A large screen had been set up. A couple of men were rigging up some kind of fancy projector. Julius Newbury, Ada's husband, stood by the side, reading from a stack of index cards.

Barb Norton called the meeting to order.

"Julius Newbury is going to answer all your questions," she said simply. "I hope you will maintain some decorum this time."

There was a smattering of applause, accompanied by a wisecrack or two from the crowd. Jenny and the Magnolias sat in the second row. Jenny had heard a lot about the uses of medical marijuana. She was eager to see what the Newburys had to say in their defense.

Lights were dimmed and the presentation started. Julius Newbury spoke well. He walked everyone through a 3D demonstration of the proposed fields and processing plant. He laid special stress on all the safety and security measures in place. A view of Main Street came up on the screen.

A murmur started going through the crowd. Julius paused the presentation and held up a hand.

"We are now going to show you the site of the dispensary itself. I know many of you have concerns about it."

The dispensary proved to be a veritable fortress. There were multiple check points to get in and get out. Employees would be scanned before they left the premises. There was no room for illicit activities.

Julius Newbury pointed to a tall, hefty man who had been standing by his side all this time. He was introduced as the security chief.

"This man has been hired to oversee the complete security of the project. Every inch of the business, whether it is the fields, the processing plant or the dispensary itself will be closely monitored by top notch security measures. The chief is here to address your concerns."

People stood up and started firing questions. The man known as 'Chief' calmly answered all of them. The crowd finally simmered down. There was a lull for a few moments. Then a woman stood up at the back.

"What about the psychological impact your drugs will have on our kids? We are teaching them it's okay to consume psychoactive drugs like cannabis? What is the message we are giving out here?"

Julius Newbury bit his lip and tried to hide his frustration.

"Your kids need to be smart enough to understand the difference. Taking a drug for a medical purpose is different from getting stoned."

"But they are too young to know the difference," another man shouted.

"That's exactly why this will never work," a voice said from the back.

"I can't discipline your kids," Julius Newbury said, turning red. "That's your job. If they are going to get into drugs, they will do it with or without my dispensary."

"What about the fields?" a woman with a baby in her arms asked. "Kids can get in there anytime."

The security chief spoke up.

"No, they can't. We have electric fences around the fields. Anyone trying to scale the fences will be electrocuted."

"You would do that to a child?" a woman asked, looking horrified.

Barb Norton stepped in before any further chaos ensued.

"We have all had our say, Julius. It's up to them now." She turned toward the crowd and pointed at Heather. "If you still want to protest this business, please sign the petition. We are going to see to it that marijuana licenses are not granted for Pelican Cove."

She looked at Julius Newbury and shrugged.

"Nothing personal, Julius."

The Magnolias helped Jenny clear up after the meeting. They took all the leftovers to Seaview for an impromptu dinner party. Jason had fired up the grill on the patio.

"The steaks are ready to go on the grill," he told Jenny.

Everyone relaxed with a drink.

"The crab salad was gone in minutes," Star said. "I'm glad we at least get to taste these pimento cheese sandwiches."

Heather's smile slipped when Adam arrived.

"Relax," he said, putting a hand on her shoulder. "I'm just here for dinner."

"It will be over soon, sweetie," Jenny promised Heather.

She wondered if she was making an empty promise. Adam stuck around after everyone had gone home. He loaded the dishwasher while Jenny put the leftovers in the fridge.

"How about a walk?" he asked.

Tank fetched a stick from the garden and dropped it at Jenny's feet.

"I guess we are going for a walk," Jenny laughed.

"What's on your mind?" Jenny asked after they had walked a quarter mile away from the house.

"More bad news," Adam said quietly. "One of Gianni's neighbors has come forward. He saw Heather leaving Gianni's house at 5 AM."

Jenny stared at Adam, her fear clearly written on her face.

"That doesn't sound good."

Adam shook his head. "It places Heather at the scene of the crime. I'm sorry, Jenny."

Jenny spent a sleepless night worrying about Heather. She was so disturbed she almost burnt a pan of muffins while making breakfast.

She finally called the Bayview Inn at 7 AM.

"I need to talk to you, Heather," she burst out. "Can you come here right now?"

Heather came in ten minutes later, looking worried.

"What's so urgent, Jenny? I was serving breakfast at

the inn."

Jenny led Heather out on the deck.

"We never talked about that night," Jenny began.

"I don't remember much, Jenny. I already told you that."

"That's not going to help you, Heather. Think!"

"I remember saying goodbye to all of you at The Steakhouse. Gianni wanted a drink when we got home. I had already had too much. The next thing I remember is waking up in my own bed."

"Someone saw you walking out of Gianni's house at 5 AM."

Heather looked dismayed.

"I must have passed out."

"Was anyone else there when you reached Gianni's house?"

"I don't think so. Wait, the door was open when we got there."

"Do you mean it was unlocked?" Jenny asked. "Or was it wide open?"

"I don't know. Gianni said something about changing

the locks."

Jenny thought furiously.

"Changing the locks? That means whoever opened the door had a key."

"Tiffany had a key," Heather cried. "You think she was waiting for us there?"

"Tiffany left for Delaware after her little altercation with you."

"She could have come back?" Heather said hopefully.

"Speculation is not going to help us, Heather. Did you see her there?"

"I don't remember."

"That's your answer to everything."

"I've never been so drunk in my life, Jenny. And I'm paying for it now."

"Gianni was bad for you, Heather."

"I know that now, when it's too late. I guess I just latched on to him on the rebound."

"After dating a dozen other guys?" Jenny's disdain was clear. "Why were you taking antidepressants, Heather?"

"You know about that?" Heather asked.

"The police know about it too. It's another factor against you."

"I wasn't doing well, Jenny. All those guys I dated were just a ruse. I was all torn up inside. I couldn't sleep. Old Dr. Smith prescribed those pills. They were a life saver."

"Did you ever give them to Gianni?"

"Of course not," Heather denied. "He didn't even know I was taking those pills."

"When did you really find out he had a wife?" Jenny gave Heather a stern look. "Was it really at The Steakhouse?"

Heather was quiet for a while. Unfortunately, she looked guilty.

"Gianni never told me about his wife. But I was beginning to have doubts. There were small signs – scent of perfume in the air, a lipstick in the medicine cabinet. I knew there was another woman. I just never dreamed he was a married man."

"Weren't you mad when you found out?"

"I was pretty mad," Heather said, remembering. "He had been talking about taking me to the Caribbean, having a dream wedding. He was a cheat and a liar."

"Why did you fight with Tiffany at the restaurant then? She was the wife. You were the other woman, Heather."

"I don't know what came over me," Heather confessed. "And I was drunk. Less drunk than I was later, but drunk enough."

"None of these things will work in your favor," Jenny said sadly.

"Is there no hope for me?" Heather wailed again.

"Go to some quiet place, clear your mind and try to remember anything you can about that night. Your life depends on it, sweetie."

"I need your help, Jenny. You helped catch so many murderers in the past. Can't you do the same this time?"

"I'm trying my best," Jenny assured her. "Meanwhile, you need to be brave. We will try to bail you out if they take you in."

Jenny's fears proved to be true. The Magnolias were sitting out on the deck later when Adam arrived with his deputies. He arrested Heather for the murder of Dr. Gianni Costa.

Betty Sue Morse was in shock. She fainted without a word, her face falling flat on the wooden table. Star fanned her with a paper napkin while Petunia loosened the buttons at her throat. Molly was about to leave to get the doctor when Betty Sue opened her eyes. She was inconsolable.

"You need to be strong, Betty Sue," Jenny told her firmly. "I'm going to get Jason. We will have Heather back here soon."

Jason was out of town on business and unreachable. Jenny left several messages, urging him to get back to town immediately. It was afternoon by the time he came back.

"I had an idea this was coming," he told Jenny. "Don't worry, I already have the papers ready. She should be out soon."

Adam sat in his office with an inscrutable expression on his face. Jenny pushed open the door and went in, ready to give him a piece of her mind.

"Believe it or not, I'm just doing my job," he sighed. "If I don't do it, someone else will."

Jenny's anger deflated like a balloon.

"This is hard on all of us," she told him. "Dr. Smith gave Betty Sue a sedative. Her blood pressure shot up. Star is sitting by her side, keeping her company."

"Has anyone else come forward?" Jenny asked. "What about any new evidence?"

Adam shook his head. "You were looking at Gianni's old files, weren't you?" Adam asked. "Why don't you go through them again? Your out of the box approach is Heather's only hope now, Jenny."

"You are actually encouraging me to keep on digging?" Jenny asked wondrously. "That doesn't sound like you."

"What are you going to do next, Jenny?" Adam asked.

"I don't know. I'm plum out of ideas."

Chapter 16

Jenny was lost in thought as she mixed the batter for banana nut muffins. She remembered how Heather had appeared on the deck one day with Gianni Costa. He had already set up his clinic in Pelican Cove at that time.

"You found Gianni on that dating site, didn't you?" she asked Heather later that morning.

"Yes, I found his profile attractive. I didn't know he lived right here."

"Did he ever talk about his earlier life? Like where he went to college or medical school?"

"He had a bunch of certificates up on the wall in his office," Heather said with a shrug. "But I never paid much attention to them."

"I think we need to find out more about Gianni," Jenny declared. "What do his patients say about him, for example? Did any of them catch on to his scams?"

"Aren't there websites where people post reviews on doctors?" Molly asked. "Doctors have a score based on the ratings patients assign them."

"I generally check those scores before going to any

specialist," Jenny nodded. "Looks like I have some work to do on the Internet."

Jenny went straight home after work that day and started her laptop. Her search yielded surprising results. Gianni had been popular with his patients. Most people had written glowing reviews about how gracious the doctor was, and how he actually listened to them. Some even went on to say he was the best doctor they had ever come across.

Jenny decided Gianni had paid someone to write fake reviews. Then she looked a bit closer. The reviews started two years ago. There wasn't a single review for Dr. Gianni Costa before that. It was almost as if he hadn't existed.

She dialed Tiffany's number.

"Hey Tiffany, got a few minutes?"

"What do you need?" Tiffany asked rudely.

She was in a bad mood.

"You don't sound so good."

"The authorities have frozen all of our bank accounts. I don't have five dollars for a cup of coffee."

"What? I am so sorry to hear that."

"What did you tell them, Jenny?" Tiffany shrieked over the phone. "What am I going to do now?"

Jenny was glad. It seemed that the authorities were pursuing other lines of investigation. That was good news for Heather.

"I'm sure it's just temporary," Jenny tried to placate her.

"Are you calling to gloat?"

"No, of course not! I had a few questions about Gianni. Do you know how long he had been living in Delaware when you met him?"

"Didn't he always live there?" Tiffany asked.

"Apparently not. Did he move there from some other part of the country?"

"If he did, he never told me about it."

"What about medical school?"

"What is this, an inquisition? There's a bunch of certificates hanging up on the wall in his clinic. I never really noticed them."

"Can you do me a favor?" Jenny pleaded. "Can you take some photos of all those certificates and send them to me? It might be important."

"Why should I do that?" Tiffany demanded. "The police confirmed my alibi for the night Gianni died. I'm in the clear."

"You won't have access to your money until the case is solved. You want that, don't you?"

"Whatever!" Tiffany said churlishly. "I guess I can take a few photos."

"Thank you. Thank you so much, Tiffany."

Jenny tapped her foot and stared at her phone every few seconds. She hoped Tiffany would send the photos right away. She didn't relish the thought of having to plead with the woman again. Jenny was just about to go out in the garden to get some fresh air when her phone pinged.

She connected her phone to her computer and downloaded the photos Tiffany had sent. Jenny was surprised to see Gianni had graduated from a prestigious medical school in the area. Why had he set up his clinic in small towns with a degree like that? He could have had a job at the finest city hospitals.

Jenny didn't have much luck when she called the medical school office. Any information about students was private. She could get a transcript if she was a prospective employer. Otherwise she had nothing.

Jenny sat on her patio, breathing in the scent of the

roses, staring at the gurgling water fountain. She remembered all the alumni association meetings her ex-husband had gone to every year. She went in and opened her laptop again. She had some calls to make.

Adam grinned from ear to ear when he spotted Jenny on the beach that night. Tank was running in circles around her, nudging her with a stick in his mouth. Jenny took the stick and threw it in a wide arc. Tank leapt after it with a joyous bark.

"I didn't get any complaints about you today so I am guessing you are staying out of trouble."

"Not exactly," Jenny confessed.

She thought of the talking down she had received from some of the men she had called earlier. She decided to keep it to herself.

"I thought the twins were bent on giving me a hard time, but you take the cake, Jenny."

"I'm doing it for a good cause," Jenny said woodenly.

"So are you going to tell me about it?"

"I tried to reach some of Gianni's friends. I looked up his alumni association and called a few people. None of the people I talked to remember him."

"I have never spoken to a single person I went to

college with," Adam grumbled. "I doubt any of them will remember me."

"I'm sure plenty of them will," Jenny argued. "You are not easily forgettable."

"That's not the point, Jenny," Adam sighed. "Not every person is a member of their alumni association."

"My ex went to every alumni function."

"You're saying Gianni didn't."

"I don't care if he was a member," Jenny said. "I'm saying no one remembered him."

"How many people did you talk to?" Adam asked.

"Plenty," Jenny said with a grimace. "All of them were from his graduating class. None of them remembered a fellow student called Gianni Costa."

Adam was quiet for a few minutes.

"You're saying Gianni put up a fake degree in his office."

Jenny shrugged.

"He could have easily forged a document."

"I think you are shooting in the dark," Adam said bluntly. "Are you saying Gianni wasn't really a doctor?"

"I don't know what to make of it," Jenny said glumly.

"You've done all you could for Heather," Adam consoled her. "I think you should let the police do their work now. I would focus on getting her a good lawyer."

"Are you saying I should just give up?" Jenny's temper flared. "Jason would never tell me that."

"I'm not Jason," Adam said haughtily. "Don't ever confuse me for him, Jenny."

"How could I? You don't have a kind bone in your body, Adam Hopkins!"

Jenny whirled around and stomped back to Seaview. Tank followed her for a while and then turned back when Adam whistled at him.

"Gianni was a doctor alright," Jason said when Jenny visited him the next morning.

She had told him about her latest theory. Jenny had been mollified when Jason didn't reject it outright.

"Think of the scam he was running," Jason mused, scratching his chin.

He had day old stubble and his eyes were red. Jenny

hoped he wasn't staying awake thinking about Kandy.

"Couldn't anyone have done it?" she asked.

"We can talk to Dr. Smith about this if you want. The scam Gianni was running required advanced knowledge about medicine and the system. Only an experienced doctor could have done it."

"Why would he put up fake credentials?"

"Because he didn't want to use his real ones?" Jason guessed.

"Wait a minute, could he have lost his license?"

"That's possible," Jason nodded. "He might have practiced in some other state before he got here."

"You won't believe it, but he has some great reviews from patients. But they only go back two years."

"What?" Jason started.

He looked at Jenny with wide eyes.

"What if it's not just the wrong medical school? What if it's the wrong person?"

"What do you mean, Jason?" Jenny asked, her heart speeding up.

"Gianni Costa could be a fake identity, Jenny. We

don't know how long he was running his scams. Maybe he moved from state to state and took up a different name every time."

"New name, new credentials and new women," Jenny said softly.

"Didn't you say Tiffany came from a simple background? That's why he must have chosen her. He wanted someone who would be wowed by his money and wouldn't ask too many questions. He just wanted a wife to look respectable."

"What about Heather?"

"He needed her to build some credibility in Pelican Cove."

"Why did he get greedy, opening a clinic in two states at a time?"

Jason shrugged.

"Maybe he wanted to retire early? It's also the unique position of the Shore. He could easily live in two places at once."

"Heather dodged a bullet," Jenny said.

"We don't know what he was planning for her," Jason said seriously.

"Should we tell Adam? He's going to call this farfetched."

"Let me take care of it, Jenny. We need Adam's help to investigate further."

Jenny's phone rang, interrupting them. Her face lit up when she saw who was calling.

"It's Nick," she smiled.

"When are you coming home, Nicky?" she asked.

Jason looked on indulgently while Jenny spoke to her son. In his late forties, Jason had given up any hopes of ever being a father. But he loved watching the special bond Jenny shared with her son.

"He's coming home tonight," Jenny said happily as soon as she hung up.

Then her face clouded over. "He has something to tell me."

"Relax. I am sure it's good news."

"You will come to dinner tonight, won't you?" Jenny said briskly. "I'm going to make Nick's favorites."

"I don't want to intrude."

"Of course you won't be intruding. Star and Jimmy will

be there too."

"Let me bring the wine then," Jason said.

Jenny had a huge smile on her face as she worked through her chores. She rubbed the charms around her neck, thinking of her son. She fired off a quick message to him around lunch time, warning him to drive slowly.

"Why don't you go home early?" Petunia said after they had lunch. "I can wrap up around here."

"Thanks," Jenny said.

She drove to the seafood market and picked up the catch of the day. She was planning to make Nick's favorite fried potatoes with fresh rosemary from her herb garden.

She had barely finished unloading the groceries at home when Nick arrived. He gave her a bear hug and allowed her to kiss him.

"You look scruffy," she said. "You do take a shower now and then?"

"Mom!" Nick complained. "I had a paper due today. I hit the road as soon as I turned it in."

"I'm so happy to see you, Nicky."

Jenny poured fresh squeezed lemonade in two tall glasses. She had muddled some strawberries and basil into them.

Nick drained half the glass in one gulp.

"I miss your cooking, Mom."

"Stop flattering me and tell me what you wanted to talk about."

She and Nick were sitting on a couch in the family room.

"I'm going to Europe in the summer," Nick said. "It's for a class."

"That's great," Jenny exclaimed. "You were so young when we took you there the last time. Hey, maybe I can join you when you're done."

"There's more," Nick said, making a face. "Dad's meeting me there. He's planned a road trip for the two of us."

"That's good for you," Jenny said, trying to hide her disappointment. "I'm glad your dad wants to spend some time with you."

Chapter 17

The Magnolias were enjoying their usual coffee break on the deck of the Boardwalk Café.

"Do you have any new leads?" Heather asked Jenny.

"I'm working on something."

That's all Jenny would say. She didn't want to reveal too much unless she was sure it was going to work in their favor.

"How's your little project with Barb Norton coming along?"

"Almost everyone in town has signed the petition. Over 90% of the people have said no to that dispensary. I think the Newburys are going to be disappointed."

"I feel bad for the people who really need that medicine," Jenny said. "But I guess some of the concerns people raised are real too."

Jenny packed a couple of chocolate cupcakes in a box and took them over to Jason. He loved chocolate.

"How are you, Jenny?" he asked, lighting up as he opened the box she handed over.

"Have you talked to Adam yet?" Jenny asked. "What does he say about our theory?"

"You know Adam," Jason shrugged. "He said he'll work on it. We have to give him a couple of days before we press any further."

"He's had his two days," Jenny fumed. "Time's running out."

Jason licked chocolate frosting off a fork and nodded.

"What do you want to do?"

"Let's go talk to him now."

Adam frowned when Jenny entered his office.

"I'm busy now. Come back later."

"We just need a few minutes, Adam."

She sat down and Jason followed.

"Did you find out anything more about Gianni?"

"Not yet," Adam admitted. "I'm drawing a blank."

Jenny leaned forward, her eyes shining with an idea.

"What if you ran his fingerprints? Have you done that yet? He might have a criminal record."

"Let me get back to you on that," Adam promised.

He ushered them out of his office, looking irritated. Jenny walked out, feeling hopeful.

"If Gianni was going around using a false identity, we will find that out soon enough."

"Fingers crossed, Jenny," Jason said, heading back to his office.

Jenny went back to the café. She had a big order for a birthday cake. She needed to start baking if she wanted to have the cake ready on time.

Adam came to Seaview for dinner that evening. Jenny was happy to see him. She tried to forget his boorish behavior from that morning. Adam always stressed that he wanted to keep his professional life separate from his private life. Jenny decided she would try the same. She was mad at Sheriff Adam but she was happy to see her beau Adam for dinner.

"This is like an impromptu date," Adam said, handing her a bunch of roses from the garden.

Star and Jimmy had gone out for a drive.

"It's just you and me," Jenny said with a blush. "Do you want to eat out on the patio?"

"It's kind of chilly outside," Adam said, rubbing his

palms together. "I can build a fire in the pit."

They finally decided to eat in the cozy breakfast nook. Jenny lit candles and served the simple pasta dinner.

Adam dunked his crusty bread in the clam sauce and stared into Jenny's eyes.

"Do you miss having me here?"

Jenny's smile was answer enough.

"Won't be for long," Adam said cryptically.

They decided to go for a walk before dessert. Jenny went upstairs to get a wrap for herself.

"I don't want to spoil the mood but I have some more news for you, Jenny. The prints came back. They belong to a man called Joe Torres."

"What else?" Jenny asked eagerly.

"I will know more tomorrow," Adam promised.

The next day, Jenny waited impatiently to hear back from Adam. She packed some lunch for the two of them and walked over to the police station.

"I'm still working on it," Adam said, chewing on his chicken salad sandwich. "I learned a few random things but I haven't pieced it together yet."

"I'll hold on a bit longer, I guess," Jenny said reluctantly.

Heather called when Jenny was about to sit down to dinner.

"Guess who just booked two rooms at the Bayview Inn?"

"Who?" Jenny played along.

"Ann Davis and her son Ricky. They are coming here in the summer."

"So Ann wasn't kidding when she said she missed the Eastern Shore."

"Apparently not," Heather agreed. "You think they are still interested in Seaview?"

"Ann is the one who sold me the house," Jenny reminded Heather. "Keith was the one who wanted to hold on to it. But he's gone now."

"Will you invite them over?"

"I don't know, Heather, we'll see."

Jenny let Heather prattle on for some time. She was pleased to see shades of the old Heather.

"Your dinner's getting cold," Star called from the table.

Jenny giggled and hung up. She loved living with her elderly aunt. It made her feel younger and reminded her of the times she had spent summers in Pelican Cove as a teen.

Jimmy regaled them with stories of some of his tenants. With tourist season coming up, he had his work cut out for him. He fixed up all the cottages, and added a fresh coat of paint.

"Sounds like you're going to be pretty busy, Jimmy," Star said, stirring a spoon in her soup.

Jenny had made pea soup with fresh peas and mint from the garden. She paired it with lemony grilled chicken breasts in a garlic butter sauce.

"This is my usual spring routine," Jimmy shrugged. "I'm used to it."

"What do you think about taking a trip?"

"Now?" Jimmy asked. "There's no way I can get away right now."

Star said nothing and took a few bites.

"Do you need to go somewhere?" Jimmy asked a few minutes later.

"Frank had this great idea," Star hesitated. "Spring time is really beautiful in the mountains."

"But your specialty is seascapes," Jimmy pointed out. "That's what the tourists buy year after year."

"I know. But a mountain landscape would be a great addition to my work. Frank says a diverse portfolio makes the artist look more experienced."

"He would know."

"Of course he does," Star said. "He's painted mountains, deserts, canyons and beaches in every possible season. I trust his opinion."

"What are you saying?" Jimmy asked quietly.

"It's a three day trip. That gives us four or five plein air sessions. I can book a room in town and drive up into the mountains in Frank's bus every day."

"Doesn't sound like you need me there," Jimmy grumbled.

Star grasped his hand.

"Of course I need you, Jimmy. It will be fun."

"You really want to do this?" Jimmy asked.

"I've been painting the ocean and the salt marshes for years. I like the thought of trying my hand at something new."

"Let me think about it," Jimmy said.

"You're going anyway, aren't you?" Jenny asked her aunt later.

"Frank's a talented artist. I can learn a lot from him."

"Is that all?" Jenny asked. "I think you have a tiny crush on him."

Star refused to comment on that. Jenny hoped her aunt would decide not to go on the trip. She wasn't too keen on sending her off with a stranger.

Jenny spent another busy day at the café, working on a few special orders. Barb Norton came in during lunch. She tasted the chicken noodle soup Jenny placed before her and pronounced it delicious.

"What brings you here, Barb?" Jenny asked, setting down a plate of crab salad with the fat free crackers Barb preferred.

"Sit down, Jenny," Barb ordered. "Spring Fest is just a few weeks away. Have you thought about it yet?"

"I guess we'll put up something just like last time."

"You haven't signed up for it yet," Barb admonished. "I need to have your final menu by the end of the week. I am going to review all of them. I might ask you to make a few changes."

Jenny mumbled something under her breath.

"We don't want everyone offering the same thing," Barb said. "If you are working on any new recipes for the festival, arrange a tasting session in the next two days."

"That's not enough time," Jenny protested.

"Serve it at the café that day," Barb ordered. "I'm sure you can do it."

Barb gave Jenny a few more pointers about the upcoming festival while she ate her lunch.

"It's hard to choose between your cupcakes or donuts," Barb said. "No waffles. We'll have funnel cakes."

Jenny finally got a chance to eat her own lunch. Jason rushed in when she had barely taken two bites.

"Adam wants us," he said.

"Can I finish eating?" Jenny asked. "I'm starving."

"Sure. I'll join you if you have another of those." Jason looked greedily at the sandwich she was eating.

They scarfed down their food in a few minutes and started walking toward the police station.

Adam was just finishing his own lunch. He tossed everything in a trash can and turned around to beam at them.

"I have some news."

Jenny's neck muscles were taut with tension.

"Good news or bad news?"

"Relax, Jenny, this will take a while."

Adam handed over a bottle of cold water. Jenny guzzled the water and looked questioningly at Adam.

"Your hunch paid off. Joe Torres, Dr. Joe Torres, lived in a small town in New Mexico. He was arrested for medical fraud."

Jenny slammed her fist on Adam's desk.

"That's more like it. What else did you find out?"

"I talked to my counterpart over there," Adam explained. "Gianni, or Joe, whatever you call him, was one of the top doctors in the town. He had been running scams for years."

"What kind of scams?" Jason asked.

"Wrong diagnoses, double billing, there's a long list. He finally got caught. One of his patients reported him and he was arrested. But they never found enough evidence to convict."

Jenny sucked in a breath.

"He must have been tipped off."

"That's what they think," Adam agreed. "The charges didn't stick so they had to let him go. His reputation suffered though and he lost his medical license."

"That must have been a big blow," Jason said. "What did he do after that?"

Adam shrugged.

"They didn't exactly keep tabs on him. There is no record of him after that."

"So Dr. Joe Torres just disappeared?" Jenny pressed.

"Something like that, Jenny. There is no address for him in that town so all we can surmise is he went somewhere else."

"He took on a new identity," Jenny said. "But the question is, how many other identities did he have before becoming Gianni Costa."

"Does that matter?" Adam asked.

"We don't know how many people he hurt," Jenny

pointed out. "If we want to find these people, we need to track down everything Gianni or Joe did."

"She has a point," Jason said, backing Jenny up.

"That's like looking for a needle in a haystack," Adam sighed.

"Are you up for the challenge?" Jenny asked him.

"We can't be sure this has any relevance to the current crime," Adam said stodgily. "It's not my job to uncover the fraud he did."

"Are you going to throw Heather under the bus just because you can't do your due diligence?"

Jenny stood with her hands on her hips and glared at Adam.

"Be careful, Jenny. I don't care for your allegations."

"Neither does Heather," Jenny snapped. "Heather may not have an alibi but I know in my heart that she is innocent."

"You're talking like the amateur you are," Adam said hotly. "Feelings don't matter in an investigation. We have to deal with hard facts."

"I will find hard facts for you, Adam Hopkins," Jenny challenged. "I will find facts you cannot ignore."

Chapter 18

"I always knew that man was up to no good," Betty Sue Morse declared. The Magnolias were huddled together on the deck of the Boardwalk Café. Coffee cooled in cups as the women mulled over what Jenny had just told them.

"What did Heather see in him?" Molly wondered out loud.

Heather sat with her hands in her lap, looking suitably contrite.

"What are you going to do next?" Star asked Jenny.

"I'm going to find out everything I can about this man, Joe Torres."

"You're a whiz at Internet research now, Jenny," Heather said meekly. "Let me know if I can help."

"I have something in mind for you," Jenny said cryptically.

Molly and Heather followed Jenny into the kitchen on the pretext of getting some food.

"What's the plan?" Molly asked, looking radiant in a new peach top.

She hadn't talked about Chris in a while but Jenny guessed the new couple was doing well.

"Heather needs to remember what happened that night," Jenny said.

Heather opened her mouth to protest. Jenny held up a hand.

"I know, I know, you were drunk! So this is what I propose. We are going to get you drunk again and try to retrace your steps. That might jog your memory."

"I promised myself I would never be that intoxicated again."

"You have to make an exception this time, Heather," Jenny said smoothly. "Your life may depend on it."

"So when are we doing this? Chris and I have a hot date tonight. We are going to Virginia Beach."

"Cancel that date," Jenny ordered. "We need you with us."

Molly agreed easily.

"You really think this idea will work?" Heather asked.

"We won't know until we try."

They agreed to meet at Seaview around 5 PM.

Jenny didn't get a chance to do her Internet research until she got home later that afternoon. She fired up her laptop and started running searches on Dr. Joe Torres. He turned out to be a popular doctor. But all the records she saw were about four years old. She started checking the social sites. Joe or Gianni appeared with a woman on his arm. There were several photos of them smiling and laughing together, at parties or at the beach. The woman was labeled as Maria or Maria Torres.

Jenny guessed the woman was his wife. The woman stopped appearing in the photos about five years ago. Jenny decided to dig deeper. She looked for other news in the region for those dates. She found some news items about a missing woman, none other than Maria Torres.

Maria had been on vacation with her husband when she disappeared. Her husband, a well known local doctor, had been devastated. The news articles printed Maria's life history. Maria had been born Maria Juanita Lopez Garcia. She had been the only child of aging parents. Her mother died when she was in high school. She had been working at the local gas company when Joe Torres saw her and fell in love with her.

A massive search had been mounted for Maria but she never came back. Many theories had been proposed. One of the theories accused Joe Torres of killing his wife and disposing of her body. It had been deemed fantastic by most people. Joe Torres was so popular in his town that no one had been willing to believe a word against him. Then he was arrested for fraud. He had been released later but the damage had been done. He lost his medical license.

Jenny couldn't find any references to Joe Torres after that. She figured he had simply relocated to another state and taken on a new identity.

Molly and Heather arrived before she had time to process all the information.

"What are we drinking?" Molly asked.

"You and I need to be sober," Jenny told her. "Heather's going to get drunk."

"Come on Jenny, we can at least have a cocktail each."

Heather chose her poison. They went into the kitchen and made strawberry daiquiris.

"Do you have something to nosh on?" Heather asked.

"You're on a liquid diet tonight, babe," Jenny teased. "Forget about food."

They watched a chick flick to while away the time. When Heather finally looked ready to pass out, Jenny drove them all to The Steakhouse.

"We are going to walk to Gianni's house from here," she told Heather.

Heather stumbled a few times but they reached the doctor's house twenty minutes later. Jenny had arranged for the door to be unlocked.

"This door was slightly ajar that night," Heather slurred.

They went in and sat down in the living room.

Heather looked around with bleary eyes.

"Gianni was sitting right there," she pointed at an arm chair. "There was a bottle on the coffee table."

"What kind of bottle?" Jenny asked.

"A fancy glass bottle full of a brown liquid."

"A crystal decanter?"

Heather shrugged. Then she sat up.

"There was a big sound, like someone banging into something."

"What did you do?"

Heather rubbed her eyes and looked at Jenny. She was beginning to sober up.

"I think I saw a shadow right there." She vaguely pointed somewhere off the living room. "And I definitely heard a sound in the kitchen."

"What did you do?"

"I told Gianni but he just laughed at me. Told me I was drunk."

"What did you do then?"

"Gianni was drinking from a glass. I grabbed it and took a sip. Then I blacked out."

"Do you remember when you woke up?"

Heather shook her head.

"I don't. Now can we please go home? This place is creeping me out."

"Let's go," Jenny agreed, helping Heather up from the couch.

They walked back to Jenny's car and got in. Jenny promised Heather a fresh pot of coffee and all the spaghetti she could eat.

Heather woke up with a headache the next morning. She went to the Boardwalk Café for breakfast. Jenny had promised her a cure for her hangover.

"Here you go," Jenny said, setting a plate of home fried potatoes before her. "Tell me when you are ready for eggs."

Heather polished off the big breakfast and sat back to enjoy her third cup of coffee.

"Did you remember anything else?" Jenny asked.

"I remember waking up," Heather replied. "It was dark outside. Gianni was sprawled on the couch."

Her eyes filled with panic when she realized what she had seen.

"Was he … he must have been …" she mumbled.

"Never mind that," Jenny soothed. "What did you do?"

"I felt nauseous," Heather told her. "The house was freezing. I realized the front door was wide open. I went out and stood there for a minute. Then I started walking home."

"Did you see anyone?"

"I don't think so," Heather shrugged. "I think I puked in some bushes somewhere."

"Did you see what time it was?"

Heather shook her head.

"I collapsed on my bed when I got home. The next thing I knew, Grandma was shaking me, telling me about Gianni."

Heather went back to the inn after that, ready to take a nap. Jenny called Molly at the library.

"How about a road trip?"

Molly managed to get some time off from the library and they set off.

"Have you called ahead?" Molly asked.

"I want to surprise her."

They reached the small Delaware town where Tiffany Costa lived. Jenny hoped she hadn't moved out yet. There was a small U-Hall outside the house and Tiffany stood by as two hefty teens loaded some furniture.

Tiffany didn't look too happy to see them.

"What are you doing here?" she asked when she spotted Jenny.

"Taking off somewhere?" Jenny asked sternly.

Tiffany shook her head.

"I'm free to go where I want. The police cleared me long ago."

"Based on a false alibi?"

Jenny folded her arms and stared at Tiffany.

"I don't know what you're talking about."

"You did stop at the coffee shop on the way out of town. But then you went back, didn't you?"

"I did no such thing."

Tiffany glared at Jenny, refusing to back down.

"Heather told me the door was ajar when she and Gianni reached home that night. Other than Gianni, you were the only one who had a key."

"That doesn't prove I used it."

"You were in the kitchen," Jenny went on. "Heather saw you."

Tiffany's nostrils flared and she looked away.

"I was looking for my bracelet," she finally admitted. "I must have dropped it in that house. It was five carats. I couldn't just let it go."

"So what? You went there looking for it?" Jenny scoffed. "Did you drug Gianni while you had a chance?"

"Of course not!" Tiffany cried. "I found the bracelet near the sink in the kitchen. I had taken it off earlier when I was doing the dishes."

"What did you see?"

"Nothing much," Tiffany said with a shrug. "Gianni was drinking whiskey from a decanter. Heather was passed out on the couch. I crept out of the living room. Gianni was too drunk to notice me. My car was parked two houses down. I got into it and drove back here."

"Did you stop anywhere on your way back?"

Tiffany answered in the negative. She had just wanted to get home and call it a night.

"So you could have been there all night," Jenny pointed out.

"Look, I'm going back home to my town. I am starting a new job next week. I want to forget I ever met Gianni."

"Good luck with that, Tiffany."

Jenny couldn't decide if Tiffany was just a victim or if she was guilty of drugging Gianni.

"What did you find out online?" Molly asked her on the way back home.

Jenny gave her a brief account of what she had learnt. They agreed Heather had escaped narrowly. Jenny dropped Molly off at the library and went to see Jason. She brought him up to date with everything she had found out.

"Let's go talk to Adam," he said grimly.

Adam Hopkins was in a bad mood again. He sat with his leg propped up on a table.

"Have you been doing your exercises?" Jenny asked him. "Your therapist can only do so much, Adam. You need to put in some effort yourself."

"Are you here to lecture me, Jenny?" Adam thundered. "What are you doing here?"

"Tiffany came back to Pelican Cove that night."

Jenny told him everything Tiffany had admitted to her. Adam didn't look convinced.

"Heather may have been present at the scene of the crime," Jason spoke. "But Tiffany was there too. They are equally innocent or guilty."

"We might have to bring Tiffany in," Adam said grudgingly.

"What about Gianni's or Joe's first wife?" Jenny asked. "Do you think he made her disappear?"

"You have been reading the tabloids," Adam told her. "There was never any proof of a crime."

Jenny and Jason walked out of the police station.

"Do you think they will drop the charges against Heather now?" Jenny asked.

"The case is not solved yet, Jenny. It's hard to say."

"Have you tried to reach Kandy again?" Jenny asked softly.

"She changed her number, Jenny." Jason sounded defeated. "I think I've tried enough. I'm done."

"Let's get your profile on that dating app Heather uses. She can show you the ropes."

"Isn't that where she met Gianni?" Jason quirked an eyebrow. "I'd rather be alone."

"You are not alone, Jason. We are all here for you."

Jason put his arm around Jenny and hugged her close. He wondered if she would ever take him seriously. He had waited too long to bare his heart.

Chapter 19

"Do you trust Tiffany?" Molly asked Jenny.

"I don't know what to say, Molls." Jenny was tired.

The girls had met for dinner at Jenny's place. Jenny had been so frustrated she had declared they needed a girls' night. Star, Petunia and Betty Sue were having their own little soiree at the Bayview Inn.

"I'm glad Grandma's not here," Heather said, taking a sip of her lemonade. "We can talk freely."

"What do you want to talk about?" Jenny asked her.

"I'm worried about her. What happens if they take me away again?"

"That's not going to happen."

Jenny's frustration was written clearly on her face.

"I haven't given up yet, Heather. I'm going to keep on digging."

"I am so sorry," Heather said with tears in her eyes. "I'm being a nuisance."

"We are here to take care of you," Molly said staunchly. "What are friends for?"

Jenny absentmindedly chewed on a piece of celery. She had hit a wall.

"Why don't we talk of something else?" she suggested. "I'm sick of thinking about Gianni. I keep going around in circles. It's not helping."

They tried to gossip about the people in town. They had talked about everyone in the next fifteen minutes.

"I need some fresh air," Heather said.

The girls moved out to the patio.

Molly shivered as some spray from the water fountain hit her.

"Do you think of her?" she asked Jenny. "Lily?"

The fountain stood on the spot where they had found the old skeleton.

"Every time I sit here," Jenny admitted. "I feel like she's waiting, asking for justice."

"Ann Davis is coming here in the summer," Heather told Molly.

"Ann was the last one to see Lily alive, wasn't she?" Molly asked. "Do you trust her?"

"I don't," Jenny said. "But I have no proof. Unless she

comes forward and gives a confession, we are at an impasse."

"Looks like Lily is never going to get her justice," Molly observed.

The next day brought some surprising developments.

Adam called Jenny at the café.

"Can you come down to the station now?"

Jenny hoped they hadn't found any more evidence against Heather. Adam was waiting for her impatiently.

"Sit down, Jenny."

Adam's eyes shone with excitement. He had never been that eager to tell her anything. He pulled out a plastic evidence bag from a drawer and slapped it on the table before Jenny.

"What's this?"

"Startling developments in the Lily Davis case. They found this in the ground with the skeleton."

A ruby ring sparkled in the plastic bag. It was set in gold and had tiny diamonds surrounding it.

"Is it real?" she asked.

"Doesn't matter," Adam said. "It's a clue, Jenny. It

could be vital to the investigation."

"Where was it all this time?"

"Don't know," Adam shrugged. "They must have overlooked it somehow. Doesn't matter. We have it now."

"Did it belong to Lily?"

"I don't think so," Adam said. "If it was Lily's, she would have been wearing it."

Jenny finally caught on.

"You think this belongs to the person who killed Lily?"

Adam nodded vigorously.

"That's exactly what I'm thinking."

"But we don't know who this belongs to."

"Leave it to the police," Adam bragged. "Once we find out who made it, we can easily see who ordered it."

"Do you mind if I take a picture of this?"

Adam was in a benevolent mood. He told her she could take as many pictures of the ring as she wanted.

Jenny forgot all about the ring after she got back to the café. She had two birthday cakes to bake and recipes to try for the Spring Fest.

"What about the pimento cheese sandwiches you made for that meeting?" Petunia asked. "People loved those."

"We'll see what Barb thinks about them," Jenny agreed. "I still haven't decided between cupcakes and donuts. Do you think we should make a few of each?"

"That's too much work for you, Jenny." Petunia didn't talk much most of the time but Jenny valued her advice.

"Maybe we should toss a coin," she laughed nervously.

"The people are going to love either," Petunia assured her.

Jenny was in a rare mood the next morning. She made cheese and pimento muffins along with crab omelets for breakfast. She couldn't wait to hear what the Magnolias thought of the savory muffins.

"Delicious," Molly pronounced with her mouth full. "You need to take a picture of this and put it on social media, Jenny."

"Oh, that reminds me," Jenny said, slapping the table with her palm.

She pulled out her phone from her apron pocket.

"What have you got there?" Betty Sue inquired as she looked up from her knitting.

Jenny stuck her phone in Betty Sue's face.

"Does this look familiar?"

Betty Sue's face was blank for a moment. She took the phone and adjusted her glasses. She peered at the picture with a frown. A minute later, her face cleared and an expression of incredulity came over it.

"Where...where did you get this, girl?"

"Do you recognize it?" Jenny asked eagerly.

Betty Sue was the first person Jenny went to when she had a question about the town. Betty Sue had been born there and had been around the longest. There wasn't much that slipped Betty Sue's notice in the town of Pelican Cove.

"It's a family heirloom," Betty Sue rasped. "Where did you get this?"

"Whose family?" Jenny gasped.

"The Davis family," Betty Sue said, sitting up. "This ring is over two hundred years old. It has been passed down in the family from generation to generation."

"So it's Lily's ring?"

Jenny tried to hide her disappointment.

"Are you listening to me, girl?" Betty Sue thundered. "Lily may have been born a Davis, but this ring wasn't meant for her. It was handed over to a bride coming into the family."

"What if there were many brides?" Heather asked.

"Then the oldest one got it, of course," Betty Sue snapped.

Jenny was busy making some calculations in her head.

"So you're saying this ring belongs to Ann Davis?"

"Sure does, or did," Betty Sue said confidently. "Although now that I think about it, I don't think she was wearing it last summer."

"No, she wasn't," Jenny said jubilantly.

She leapt to her feet and whirled around.

"I have to go."

"Wait a minute," Betty Sue called out. "Tell me more about this."

Jenny was already down the café steps before Betty Sue could finish her sentence. She almost jogged down the boardwalk and headed to the police station. Nora, the desk clerk waved her through.

Adam was in a meeting with a bunch of other uniformed men when Jenny burst into his office.

"How about knocking before you enter?" he asked irritably.

"It's Ann. It's Ann Davis."

"What is?"

"The ring, Adam. The ring is a Davis family jewel and it belonged to Ann Davis. Betty Sue will vouch for it."

Adam's face broke into a smile.

"Leave the rest to me, Jenny."

Jenny walked back to the café slowly, wishing for a breakthrough in Gianni's case. The Magnolias were waiting with their questions.

"That ring was found in the dirt that came with the skeleton," she told them. "Or something like that."

"What was Ann's ring doing there?" Star asked.

"That's what the police will look into now," Jenny explained. "If you ask me, it puts her on the spot."

"Why would Ann harm Lily though?" Molly asked in a puzzled voice.

"She's the only one who can tell us that."

Betty Sue's eyes had filled up.

"Lily looked up to her. She was like the older sister she never had."

"An older sister who stabbed her in the back?" Heather scoffed.

"The ring doesn't prove anything. Ann can spin any story now. I don't think she will confess after all these years."

Jenny was proven wrong.

Ann Davis unraveled like a ball of string when she saw the ring.

"She said it was an accident," Adam told her as they walked on the beach. "She didn't mean to hurt Lily."

"Why did they get into a fight?" Jenny wanted to know.

"Lily had been acting crazy," Adam explained. "Those were Ann's words. She wanted to sell Seaview for a pittance. She just wanted to get away from Pelican Cove."

"Ann wasn't ready to sell?"

"She wanted Seaview for her son."

"They fought over a piece of land?"

"That wasn't all," Adam continued. "Lily barely spoke to anyone for months. She shut herself in her room, mourning her daughter. Ann got friendly with Lily's husband. They might have had an affair."

"How dare she!" Jenny cried.

Jenny's husband had dumped her after falling in love with a much younger woman. She didn't think kindly about women who wrecked other women's homes.

"Ann didn't admit to the affair," Adam said. "She just told us they had a big argument. It got a bit violent. Ann pushed her and Lily struck her head on a stone in the garden. She died instantly."

"What if Ann was mistaken?"

"She must have tried to revive her," Adam shrugged. "We will never know that."

"So Ann decided to bury her in the garden?"

"Ann says she panicked. Ricky had watched everything from an upstairs room. Lily's son was expected back home any moment. She told Ricky to start digging."

"Didn't the son or husband notice anything amiss in

the garden?"

"Ann made up that story about seeing Lily get in the car with a man. Keith was devastated when he thought his mother abandoned him."

Jenny had met Lily's son when he came to Pelican Cove. She knew he had been traumatized by his mother's actions.

"So she not only killed Lily, she also maligned her character." Jenny thought of the petite old woman she had met a few months ago. She would never have guessed she was a murderer.

"What happens now?" Jenny asked.

"Ann Davis and her son will both face charges," Adam told her.

Jenny couldn't wait to meet the Magnolias the next morning.

"I knew Lily would never turn her back on her family," Betty Sue said tersely. "Lily can finally rest in peace."

Jenny sat on the patio with her aunt, staring at the water fountain.

"Do you think it's true?" she asked her aunt. "What they say about Seaview?"

Star gave her a pained look.

"You're not thinking about that nonsense again?"

"Just think about it. Lily lost her daughter at a young age, she got herself killed, then her son got into drugs and he got himself killed. Her husband is barely alive in some senior home."

"No one can predict the future, honey," Star sighed. "You have made a beautiful home here for yourself. Try to stay happy in it."

"Here's to happy memories," Jenny nodded, clinking her cup of coffee with Star's.

Star gave her a curious look.

"I don't think you will be staying here much longer, anyway."

"What do you mean, Star?" Jenny laughed. "I'm not going anywhere."

Star looked at her niece indulgently.

"I think Adam's getting ready to pop the question."

Jenny blushed furiously.

"You do love him?" Star asked.

Jenny's eyes clouded with confusion.

235

"Is love enough?" Jenny asked moodily. "I loved Nick's father with all I had. Look where that got me."

"It will be different this time," Star said, patting her on the back.

"Do you approve?" Jenny asked her aunt.

"You know I like Jason more," Star winked. "But I'm with you, baby. I can't imagine being alone in this big old house though."

Jenny shook her head.

"Like I said, I'm not going anywhere."

Chapter 20

Jenny sipped her coffee quietly as the Magnolias chatted around her. Heather was giving them an update on Barb Norton's latest project. The signatures she had collected from the town people had done the job. The Newburys had not been granted the approvals they needed to set up the medical dispensary.

Heather's face was animated as she narrated what had happened. She seemed to have found a new purpose while working for Barb. But the cloud of suspicion still hung over her. Was Heather guilty after all? She had been the woman scorned.

Jenny's mind wandered as she imagined what Heather must have felt when she realized Gianni was already married. She must have been ready to bash someone's head in. Jenny chided herself for thinking the worst of her friend. There had been no new developments. The police still considered Heather their top suspect.

Jenny scratched her head and wondered what more she could do. She needed to start from scratch and go over everything with a fine-tooth comb.

"Thinking about Adam?" Molly asked with a glint in her eye.

Molly and Chris were very happy together. They felt

everyone around them needed to be in a relationship.

"Come with me," Jenny said suddenly. "If you can take some time off, that is."

Molly sensed the urgency in Jenny's voice.

"Sure, Jenny, let me make a call."

Jenny started walking toward Dr. Smith's clinic.

"What are we doing?" Molly wanted to know.

"You're good at research, aren't you? I need a pair of sharp eyes."

Jenny spoke to Dr. Smith and asked for the patient records from Gianni's clinic. He pointed them to a small room at the back.

"See those four boxes?" he said. "Have at it."

"We are going to go over these again," Jenny told Molly.

"But what are we looking for?"

"Anything unusual?" Jenny shrugged. "I'm not sure, Molly. We are looking for a needle in a haystack, anything that can take the limelight away from Heather."

Jenny noticed Dr. Smith had marked some of the files.

He had written remarks in the margins like 'fake diagnosis', 'wrong prescription' etc.

Molly turned out to be more efficient than Jenny. She got through a box much faster than Jenny and arranged the papers in neat piles.

"I know most of these people," Molly told Jenny. "Some are friends or acquaintances, others just sound familiar. But there's a bunch of names that don't seem to be from around here."

"They might belong to his patients in Delaware," Jenny mused. "Or they might be fictitious names. Gianni billed the government for nonexistent patients."

"What do you want to do with those?"

"Keep them in a separate pile," Jenny said thoughtfully. "I want to go through them."

The piles grew as Jenny and Molly worked through the boxes. Jenny finally turned to the pile Molly had set aside as out-of-towners. She read each file carefully, paying special attention to the names. One name caught her eye right away.

"Why does this sound familiar?" she wondered out loud. "Francis Lopez."

"Never heard of him," Molly shrugged.

The girls worked diligently for a couple of hours without much success.

"I don't know about you, Jenny, but I'm starving."

"Let's go grab a bite at the café."

They weren't in the best of spirits when they went back to the café.

"No luck?" Petunia asked sympathetically.

She placed two plates of chicken salad sandwiches before them and ladled tomato soup in earthen mugs.

"Do you know someone called Francis?" Jenny asked Petunia.

"Doesn't ring a bell," the older woman said, shaking her head. "Why don't you ask Betty Sue? She's coming here for lunch today."

Betty Sue walked in with Heather following close behind. Heather was carrying their black poodle Tootsie in her arms.

"I'll tie her out on the beach," she told Petunia immediately. "She didn't want to stay back home."

Everyone moved out to a table on the deck. Betty Sue sipped her soup and looked hopefully at Jenny.

"How's it going? Any luck?"

Jenny sighed in frustration.

"I feel I'm close, Betty Sue. But I feel I'm forgetting something."

Betty Sue had never heard of Francis Lopez either. Heather had been sitting on the café steps, playing with Tootsie. She looked up sharply.

"Isn't that the artist your aunt is going around with?"

"My aunt is not going around with anyone other than Jimmy," Jenny said sharply.

"Pay attention, Jenny," Heather pressed. "Frank Lopez? He's that new artist."

Jenny felt a chill run down her spine. She looked around at her friends.

"You think Frank Lopez is Francis Lopez?"

The ladies shrugged.

"I need to talk to Adam right away," Jenny cried, springing to her feet.

She skipped down the steps and hurried down the beach to the police station. Nora, the desk clerk, waved her through.

"Have you brought my lunch, Jenny?" Adam asked with a smile.

"Frank Lopez!" she panted. "You need to bring him in."

"Stop screaming in my ear, Jenny. I haven't had lunch yet."

"Didn't you hear what I said?" Jenny asked, putting her hands on her hips.

"You're always making outlandish demands. Now sit down and tell me what's going on."

"I think Frank Lopez is our guy. You need to bring him in right away."

"Who is he?"

"He's that new artist in town. Don't you remember?"

"And why should I arrest him?" Adam asked patiently.

Jenny launched into what she had been doing all day. She reminded him about the woman who had been Gianni's wife a few years ago.

"I think this guy is related to that girl Maria. There has to be a connection."

"Sounds farfetched to me," Adam shook his head.

"What is this Frank Lopez doing in Pelican Cove, Adam? Why is he here now?"

"We have absolutely no proof he knew Gianni."

"He was Gianni's patient. That's your connection."

Adam finally decided to humor Jenny.

"I'll send a car out to bring him in."

Jenny thanked Adam and stood up. She had decided to go confront Frank herself. Adam recognized the resolve he saw in Jenny's eyes.

"Don't do anything foolish," he called out after her.

Jenny vaguely remembered Frank talking about a house he had rented in town. Her tires spun as she raced to the address. She was looking for the trailer belonging to Frank. The house looked deserted when she got there. Her phone rang just then. It was Star.

"I'm sorry I couldn't say goodbye."

"What? Where are you?" Jenny asked, dazed.

"I'm with Frank. We are going to paint the mountains, remember? We talked about this."

"But I thought you weren't going."

"I'll be away for three days," her aunt said. "Frank's

trailer is just awesome, Jenny. It has a bed and a TV and a small kitchen. I'm going to have fun."

Jenny cringed as she thought of the close quarters her aunt was sharing with Frank.

"Is Frank with you?"

"Of course he is. You don't sound too good, Jenny. Are you coming down with something?"

"I just feel bad I didn't get to say bye to you," Jenny laughed nervously. "Why don't you stop at the next rest area? I'm on my way."

"Don't be silly. I'll be back before you know it."

"No, no, I insist," Jenny said in a weird voice. "It's such a beautiful day. I'm looking forward to a nice drive."

"We're twenty miles out of town," Star said. "Can you catch up with us?"

"The trailer goes slower than a car, doesn't it? I'll be there, don't worry."

"Whatever you say, my dear." Star sounded confused but Jenny was glad she was playing along.

Jenny called Adam right away.

"You need to stop them. If I'm right, Star could be in danger."

"Aren't you getting carried away?" Adam asked.

"I'm driving out to meet them," Jenny said firmly. "You can meet me there or not. I leave it up to you."

Jenny broke the speed limit trying to reach the rest area as soon as possible. Luckily, she didn't get pulled over. A car belonging to the Pelican Cove police overtook her just as she turned into the exit lane. Adam was already out of the car by the time Jenny parked next to him. A couple of deputies stood by, waiting for a signal from Adam.

Jenny spotted Star by the vending machines and ran toward her. She flung her arms around her aunt and hugged her tight.

"Thank God, you are safe."

"What's going on, Jenny?" Star asked sharply. "Are you going to tell me why you are acting like this?"

"You'll find out soon enough."

Frank walked up, holding packets of potato chips and cans of soda.

"They didn't have the diet cola so I got regular."

He smiled at Jenny.

"You can visit with your aunt as long as you want. There's no rush."

For a moment, Jenny wondered if she was wrong about Frank.

Adam had walked up to Jenny. Frank looked at the uniformed sheriff standing before him and his shoulders slumped. He dropped the food he was carrying on a bench and held up his hands.

"I'm not sorry I avenged my daughter."

Star's eyes popped open as Adam arrested Frank and took him away.

"I'm so glad you are okay, Star," Jenny said, hugging her aunt again.

The Magnolias arrived early at the Boardwalk Café the next day. Heather was grinning widely.

"Jason just called. Frank Lopez gave a full confession."

"Tell us what happened, Jenny," Betty Sue commanded. She was looking relieved, now that Heather had been vindicated of any involvement in the crime.

"I don't have all the details," Jenny began. "This is

what Adam told me at a high level. Frank's daughter Maria was married to Gianni. As far as I can tell, she was his first wife. She found out about his shady business and threatened to go to the police if he didn't clean up his act."

"So he was always crooked," Molly observed.

"Gianni promised her he would do whatever she wanted. They went on a trip after that. Maria never came back. Gianni said she walked out of the hotel room. There was a big investigation but Gianni got away because there was no evidence against him."

"Are you saying he killed that poor girl?" Petunia asked with a gasp.

Jenny nodded.

"She never surfaced anywhere else. Frank believed Gianni murdered his daughter. He hired investigators and tried hard to get Gianni convicted but he didn't succeed. Then Gianni vanished."

"How could he do that?"

"He went to a different state and took on a new identity," Jenny explained. "But he didn't change his ways. He carried out the same scams. When things got too hot, he moved and changed his name again."

"So Gianni wasn't his real name?" Heather asked.

"No, sweetie," Jenny said. "Not by a long shot."

"What do you mean, Maria was his first wife?" Star asked.

"Gianni went to small towns and wooed a local girl. He chose someone who would help him build contacts and set up his clinic. He got rid of the girl when he moved."

"So he killed more than one woman?" Heather gasped.

"That's what the police think now," Jenny told them. "We will know more after a thorough investigation."

"How did Frank know Gianni was here?" Star asked.

"Frank had been looking for Gianni ever since he disappeared. He drove around the country, following Gianni's trail. He traced him to Delaware and then to Pelican Cove. He posed as a patient and made sure Gianni was the man his daughter had been married to."

"When did he decide to murder him?" Molly asked.

"Revenge was always on his mind. Once he located Gianni, it was just a matter of when and how."

"How did he do it?" Heather asked in a hushed voice.

"That shadow you thought you saw that night," Jenny

said, "that was Frank. He got into Gianni's clinic and powdered a few drugs. He added them to the whiskey decanter, knowing Gianni would probably drink from it after coming home."

"What if I had drunk from it?" Heather cried.

Jenny shrugged.

"Frank was single minded in his determination. I don't think he cared about collateral damage."

"So I almost died too?" Heather gasped.

"You had a narrow escape, girl," Betty Sue's voice boomed. "That's what comes of associating with scum."

"But he was so nice to me!"

Heather looked shocked.

"What did Frank do that night?" Molly asked, prompting Jenny to go on.

"He just stood in the shadows and watched Gianni drink from the decanter. I think he was prepared to pour it down his throat if needed."

"I don't understand one thing," Heather said. "Why did he stick around in town after that? All he had to do was get in his bus and drive away."

Jenny looked at her aunt.

"We'll never know that, I guess."

Star looked around at the group of friends gathered around the table and shook her head.

"He was a really good artist."

Epilogue

The town of Pelican Cove was busy celebrating Spring Fest. People had turned up in droves. A big marquee had been erected. Food stalls lined one side. A band was setting up on a makeshift stage on the beach.

Jenny sat among her friends, finally catching her breath after a hectic day. All the food from the Boardwalk Café had been sold. Tourists had come to the festival especially to taste Jenny's cupcakes and pimento cheese sandwiches.

"I don't know how to thank you," Heather gushed. "You saved my life, Jenny."

"You were innocent all along," Jenny said lightly. "You had nothing to fear."

Adam Hopkins limped up to the group of women. He gulped as he tried to catch Jenny's eye. Jenny had been giving him the cold shoulder for a while.

"Go talk to that Hopkins boy," Betty Sue said, tipping her head at Adam.

Jenny stood up reluctantly and took a few steps toward Adam.

"What is it?"

"Can you spare a few minutes? Please?"

The sun was low on the horizon, painting the sky in shades of orange and mauve. Jenny accompanied Adam to the beach. He was quiet while they walked away from the crowd.

"Are you going to say anything?" Jenny prompted.

Adam cleared his throat.

"You know I'm not big on words, Jenny. But I hope you know how much you mean to me."

He pulled a small gift wrapped box out of his pocket and held it out to her.

"What's this?" Jenny asked suspiciously.

"Aren't you going to open it?"

Jenny pulled off the blue satin ribbon and tore the wrapping paper. Her heart thudded a bit as she lifted the lid of the small box. A shiny key lay inside.

"Err... what's this, Adam?"

"Jenny King, you already hold the key to my heart. This is the key to my house."

Jenny's brows settled into a frown.

"I want you to move in with me, Jenny."

Jenny stared into Adam's blue eyes. She was dismayed at the hope she saw there.

"I can't do that," she said under her breath. "I'm sorry, Adam."

"Why not?" Adam asked, trying to maintain his composure.

"I am just getting settled in at Seaview. I'm not leaving it now."

"Jenny, it's just a house."

"No, Adam. It's my home. It's where I am going to spend the rest of my days."

Adam took Jenny's hands in his.

"Will you at least think about it?"

Jenny stared into the sand at her feet. She gave Adam a slight nod. Then she turned around and started walking back to her friends.

THE END

Thank you for reading this book. If you enjoyed this book, please consider leaving a brief review. Even a few words or a line or two will do.

As an indie author, I rely on reviews to spread the word about my book. Your assistance will be very helpful and greatly appreciated.

I would also really appreciate it if you tell your friends and family about the book. Word of mouth is an author's best friend, and it will be of immense help to me.

Many Thanks!

Author Leena Clover

http://leenaclover.com

Leenaclover@gmail.com

http://twitter.com/leenaclover

https://www.facebook.com/leenaclovercozymyst
erybooks

Other books by Leena Clover

Pelican Cove Cozy Mystery Series –

Strawberries and Strangers

Cupcakes and Celebrities

Berries and Birthdays

Sprinkles and Skeletons

Muffins and Mobsters

Parfaits and Paramours

Meera Patel Cozy Mystery Series -

Gone with the Wings

A Pocket Full of Pie

For a Few Dumplings More

Back to the Fajitas

Christmas with the Franks

Acknowledgements

This book would not have been possible without the support of many people. I am thankful to my beta readers and advanced readers and all my loved ones who provide constant support and encouragement. A big thank you to my readers who take the time to write reviews or write to me with their comments – their feedback spurs me on to keep writing more books.

Join my Newsletter

Get access to exclusive bonus content, sneak peeks, giveaways and much more. Also get a chance to join my exclusive ARC group, the people who get first dibs on all my new books.

Sign up at the following link and join the fun.

Click here →
http://www.subscribepage.com/leenaclovernl

I love to hear from my readers, so please feel free to connect with me at any of the following places.

Website – http://leenaclover.com

Twitter – https://twitter.com/leenaclover

Facebook –
http://facebook.com/leenaclovercozymysterybooks

Email – leenaclover@gmail.com

Made in the USA
Middletown, DE
28 November 2023

43837801R00154